# NETWORK MARKETING
## GETTING IT RIGHT

EMBASSY BOOKS
www.embassybooks.in

NETWORK MARKETING - GETTING IT RIGHT

First Edition 2016

Published in India by:
**Embassy Books**
120, Great Western Building,
Maharashtra Chamber of Commerce Lane,
Fort, Mumbai 400 023, India
Tel: (+9122) -30967415,  22819546
Email: info@embassybooks.in
www.embassybooks.in

ISBN: 978-93-83359-44-8

Cover Design by Namrata Chattaraj

# It's Up To Me

*I get discouraged now and then*
*When there are clouds of gray,*
*Until I think about the things*
*That happened yesterday.*
*I do not mean the day before*
*Or those of months ago,*
*But all the yesterdays in which*
*I had the chance to grow.*
*I think of opportunities*
*That I allowed to die,*
*And those I took advantage of*
*Before they passed me by.*
*And I remember that the past*
*Presented quite a plight,*
*But somehow I endured it and*
*The future seemed all right.*
*And I remind myself that I*
*Am capable and free,*
*And my success and happiness*
*Are really up to me.*

*- James J. Metcalfe*

# CONTENTS

WHY READ THIS BOOK? 7

1 WELCOME TO THE BUSINESS OF HAPPINESS 13

2 DISCOVERING YOURSELF 21

3 WHY SIGN UP? 29

4 LIVE YOUR DREAMS 39

5 PROSPECTING 49

6 INVITING 59

7 SHOW THE PLAN 65

8 FOLLOW UP AND FOLLOW THROUGH 75

9 HANDLING OBJECTIONS 83

10 THE COMPOUNDING PRINCIPLE 93

11 BELIEVE AND ACHIEVE 101

12 PERSISTENCE 107

13 ATTITUDE IS EVERYTHING 113

14 THE BUSINESS OF RELATIONSHIPS 121

15 LEADING LEADERS 129

16 MENTORING 137

17 ARE YOU A GOOD NETWORKER? 145

# WHY READ THIS BOOK?

The business of network marketing is simple. Like many things in life, it looks complex until you truly understand it. People who are unsuccessful often think that success is a complicated business. The purpose of this book is to uncomplicate matters.

The chapters that follow will walk you through the essentials of network marketing and save you many years, months, and days of learning from mistakes. It is good to learn from experience, but it is even better if one can learn from the experience of others. This book aims to cut short your learning curve and give you the combined experience of millions of network marketers, distilled into short, concise tips that you can apply with ease.

## WHAT YOU CAN EXPECT FROM THIS INDUSTRY

With the principles given in this book, you will not only become a great network marketer, but you will also benefit in various other aspects of life, be it at your workplace, in your family life, or your relationships. Once you ignite the leader within you, you will see that you become a better father, a better husband, a better person within your social community, a better professional at work— in short, a better individual.

To believe in others, you have first start believing in yourself.

During networking marketing functions and meetings, I have seen children go up on stage and say that before their parents joined this business, there were fights and arguments at home which have now disappeared, and that they now have a peaceful and happy environment in the house. Children are honest, and there something to this statement, because I have heard it from a number of kids.

It is something tangible. People who have made in this industry see changes that go beyond the scope of the business. Individuals who are building their network and are still working at jobs have started taking more responsibility and assuming leadership roles in their careers, resulting in their going up the corporate ladder. Their communication skills and ability to work with teams have improved. Clients actually ask for them. Such a person can diffuse issues and handle situations. This, combined with a good ability to handle people, makes such an individual a valuable asset to any business or corporation.

When getting it right in network marketing, with the help of this book, you will see a number of other aspects of your life getting fixed. Your social skills will improve and your friendships will thrive. I have seen marriages on the brink of breaking turn back into happy relationships. So when we are speaking of getting it right we are speaking of developing an art of controlling the uncontrollable with regard to the people factor, because eventually it all boils down to people. It is not about products, finance, or service. People are what drive it all. When you can control people, you can control the rest.

## GETTING IT RIGHT

The title of this book was chosen for a purpose. Despite network marketing being an exceedingly rewarding industry, there are a large percentage of people who don't make it. They put in efforts, don't get the desired results, get frustrated, and end up saying, "This doesn't work for me." One often hears such people deriding the industry at social gatherings.

It is important to differentiate between 'more efforts' and 'right efforts.' These are two different concepts, like working hard and working smart. People often expect results with more efforts, and when it does not give them results, they either give up or give in, out of sheer frustration. They are being active, yes, but not productive.

My first advice to you is that you don't have to personally fail to learn. Learn from the mistakes of others. Imagine that you have to walk through a terrain rigged with land mines. You don't know where these land mines are planted. What would be your chances of making it to the other side? Slim. But if you had access to someone who has been walking through the terrain each day and who knew it thoroughly, your best bet would be to put each step precisely where the veteran is stepping and follow his footsteps. Welcome to the concept of duplication.

This said, while taking the benefit of experience, one also needs to keep things in perspective. For example, in a spiritual belief, is it more important to follow the religion or to follow the priest? The religion, obviously, because at the end of the day, the priest is only there to help you follow the religion. Similarly, in most network marketing companies, do you follow the leader or follow the system? Most people follow the leader without keeping the system in mind. The leader is also human and with the best of intentions, but he can also make mistakes. Follow the leader only as far as he is following the system.

The system is always above the leader, because when you correctly follow the system, you will not only be benefiting yourself, but in the long run, you will also benefit the leader you are following.

The aim here is not to scare people off; it is just to let them know that there is a 'right way' to succeed in network marketing. People may call it a secret, but fortunately there is no secret. It's simply about knowing the right practices. Often, the solutions to the problems in life are very simple; but we feel that if something is difficult, the solution must also be equally difficult. More often than not, the solution may be staring you right in the face.

For example, let's say a person buys himself a brand-new car. He has seen advertisements and has heard that it's a fantastic car. His friend has a similar model and recommends it, saying that driving it is a pleasure. So he 'signs up,' so to say, to own that car. It comes with a manual which says, "Check the tyre pressure every three weeks or every three hundred miles." Every owner who has been successfully driving that model will follow this practice. However, this person neither reads the manual nor does he ever check the tires. The next thing he knows, a few months down the line, he has a flat tire. It's not even a puncture; the tyre has simply run out of air.

We now have an upset car owner. He complains about the car, speaks badly about the model, blames the company for posting misleading advertisements about a 'maintenance free' car, and blames his best friend for recommending it. At every social gathering and on every blog, he keeps talking about his terrible experience of owning the car. He makes fun of the company and the product and tells everyone he meets what a mistake it was buying this model.

Now suppose that the same person had gone to pick up his new car along with his friend who had recommended the car and who was having such a wonderful experience owning it. The friend would have told him how to check the tyre pressure and oil levels and how to keep the car in great shape. The friend would have also shared his own knowledge with the new owner - what the various indicator lights meant, what the best way to get good mileage while driving was, and so on.

The same buyer would have had a completely different experience. He would have benefitted from the mistakes of someone who has done it all before him.

That is what we are trying to get from this book - the best practices from all the successful leaders who have been through network marketing and have recorded what works.

Now let's take a look at the business of happiness.

*Chapter 1*

# WELCOME TO THE BUSINESS OF HAPPINESS

"I expect to pass through this world but once. If therefore, there be any kindness I can show or any good things that I can do, let me do it now. Let me not deter it or neglect it for I shall not pass this way again."

**~ William Penn**

Happiness is serious business. Look around and you can see a world going about very seriously at work. You literally have to pull yourselves out of the bed in the morning, have breakfast, take a shower, catch a train or bus or drive to the office, get stuck in traffic jams, and by the time you start work you are drained of energy. This vicious cycle goes on from Monday to Friday and seems never-ending with the same routine and the same challenges. You are eagerly waiting for the weekend right at the beginning of the week itself!

And then you wish, "What if I didn't have to go through the ordeal everyday and yet earn my livelihood?" It is as if we have become robots with a heart that has forgotten to love and be happy. We have lost the humor in our lives; in fact, we barely smile. When I ask people, "When is the last time you had a hearty laugh?" they have to really scratch their heads. We have forgotten to laugh and then need to join laughter clubs as laughter is good for health.

One does encounter humor at the workplace - well, sometimes - but how often do you see people who are truly happy to be at work? I believe the problem lies more with people doing what they don't enjoy. As the saying goes, "A man who loves what he does doesn't work for a single day in his life."

Moreover, man is a social animal and hence cannot survive alone. Because of the indulgence in the rat race in today's times, we are left with no time to socialize and nurture relationships.

Wouldn't it be an ideal life where you are meeting lot of people, building lasting relationships, having enough time for yourselves and your family, and, at the same time, earning your bread and butter with a topping of jam on it?

Network marketing was started to fulfil all this. It started as a system of referrals. Business from word-of-mouth is far more powerful than any known form of advertising as it is based on trust and relationships. Direct selling companies started using referrals as a way of letting people know about their products and services. Distributors used the product or service and shared their positive experiences with others, bringing in more sales as a result. The company compensated the referring distributor on a multi-level basis, so the distributor got not only a discount on his own consumption but also got a royalty on what was consumed or sold by the person he introduced, whom we may refer to as a downline (because he is down in the line of sponsorship), and on every person that downline introduced and so on.

Thus came the term multi-level marketing. You made money on all the 'levels' that followed the person you introduced to the business. It worked on word-of-mouth and used the power of duplication of effort.

Happy users obviously make the best salespeople in the world and also are the best people to train others to sell what they believe is a great product.

The beauty of this business is that it does not require a particular kind of education or qualification, nor does it require one to be of a particular nationality, or to have any prior experience. It is a business that goes beyond the confines of national or educational boundaries. Some of the best teams in the industry are multicultural. Anyone can sign up. What's more, as soon as a distributor gets started, he would find enthusiastic people willing to teach him the ropes.

As with every business, even in network marketing, you can achieve to the point where you believe you can achieve. Another great advantage of this business is that you can do it from any place, including your home, so it is popularly known as the home-based business. It saves you the expenses of running an office (and running to the office). Running it from home also means it is easy to involve your spouse. Very soon, more and more couples started building the business as a team than any other industry. The positive effect of this was that the shared business also often contributed to building better relationships.

Once, an interesting question was raised at one of our conventions by a distributor, who asked me, "Is network marketing an art or a science?"

On the face of it, it seems to be an art, as only a few people are getting it right. Something would be an art if only a few people with exceptional abilities could excel at it. However, I believe that it is truly a science, because anyone with a good understanding of the principles and processes involved in network marketing would succeed.

But the world of science is more defined. If two molecules of hydrogen are combined with one molecule of oxygen, you will get water each and every time, regardless of who does it. It's a formula. The process can be observed and duplicated. That is what network marketing is about. It is about observing what works in the business, replicating it to attain financial freedom, and then passing it down to other people so that they can also use the good practices that you have learnt. You learn, earn, and pass it on.

Being the first point of contact between the company and your prospects, you become the brand ambassador for the business. People have to accept you before they accept the company or its products, which is why we can also call this relationship marketing. You first build a relationship, and then you market the products.

Going back to the roots of this business, it is important to share your positive experiences—the sale itself is incidental. Once you have shared your experience, you give people the time and space to take it further and reach a decision. When you watch a movie that you enjoyed, or visit a restaurant where the food and service were particularly good, you like to share your experience with your family and friends, right? You give them the opportunity to enjoy a positive experience, because you wish well for them. Once you recommend them a restaurant, you don't call them thrice a day to check if they actually watched the film or ate there!

This is not a business of just 'selling' products. It is unfortunate that due to the way some distributors have projected it, people often misinterpret it as selling. As the name states, it is a business of building a network; people like yourself who use the products and believe they as are good for others as they are for themselves. It is a business of sharing – both your positive experience as well as the opportunity to have more time and make more money.

There is one common quality which I have noticed in all successful entrepreneurs in this industry. Each of them has made it a business of goodness. Each of them had a dream which they believed in. This business is best built with innocence or, unfortunately, at times with ignorance. Once you develop the mind of an 'entrepreneur' instead of that of a 'salesman,' it will work for you. So the trick is to let the money chase you rather than you chasing the money.

Put people first. This is a people's business. Products do not create problems, people do. Just look around you and you can see this statement verified. Facts do not motivate people, emotions do. So the right way of handling people is critical to success in network marketing.

Creating the right environment for the seed of potential to germinate and become a tree that gives people the shade of security and the fruit of prosperity is the master key to success in this industry. Network marketing allows you to make friends while gaining financial freedom. And the best part is that these are your friends in the true sense of the word, because they are headed in the same direction as you and they want you to succeed as much as you want them to succeed.

The industry is based more on relationships than any other single aspect. Most network marketing companies, especially the really good ones, will have an education system. This helps you to develop not only your entrepreneurial skills but your overall persona. As you grow in the business, you will find your confidence building and your people skills getting better and better. Stay put for a while and you will soon enough discover that you have developed an ability to take a leadership position in a group. Most jobs tend to enslave you. You need to work harder and harder to make more money. As your lifestyle goes up, so does the pressure on you to keep putting in more time and effort to increase your income.

So let's move away from the 'kingdom of slaves' and take a look at the 'business of happiness.'

## TAKEAWAY

- *Network marketing is a business that goes beyond the confines of national or educational boundaries.*

- *It is a business of sharing – both your positive experience as well as the opportunity to have more time and make more money.*

- *Products do not create problems, people do. Facts do not motivate people, emotions do. So the right way of handling people is critical to success in network marketing.*

- *The industry is based more on relationships than any other single aspect.*

- *Network marketing can be summed up as learn, earn, and pass it on.*

## Chapter 2

# DISCOVERING YOURSELF

'Your task is to build a better world,' God said.
I answered, 'How?
This world is such a large, vast place, so complicated now,
And I so small and useless am
There's nothing I can do.'
But God said, in all His wisdom,
"Just build a better you."

**~ Author Unknown**

Before we step into the amazing world of network marketing, let's explore the most important aspect at the centre of this business – YOU. Network marketing is a people's business, and if you wish to succeed in this business, it is important to understand the building blocks—people, and what really motivates and inspires them.

It is said that you see your reflection in others. Therefore, the key to understanding others is to first understand yourself. Business is all about relationships, and the most important relationship you share is with yourself. Once you are in tune with your inner self, it is easy to strike a harmonious chord with the people around you. And when you build lasting and trusting relationships, business happens on its own. My business gives me an opportunity to travel across the globe and meet people with different socioeconomic and cultural backgrounds. I have observed that I can easily connect with them only if I am in sync with my own self.

To know yourself better, you need to probe deeper into yourself. Ask questions like: "Am I happy with my current situation?"

"What does my life look like at present?"

"Do I enjoy what I do?"

"Do I have a fulfilling career?"

"Am I living the lifestyle I always wanted to live?"

"Where do I stand financially?"

"And where do I see myself ten years from now?"

These questions and the answers to them will lead to three important aspects:

What is your take on finance?

What is the purpose of your life?

What is your definition of success?

Let us take a fleeting look at each one of them.

## FINANCE

When I ask people, "What do you think about money?" the following answer is quite common: "Well, I don't really care about money." I feel it is an unfounded statement. You may not really care about money, but you also cannot deny the fact that without it, you cannot have even the basic necessities of life. Although I don't care much for money, myself, I sure like the things that money can buy. We don't have to be obsessed with the commodity itself, but having money does give us more options and choices in life. Money is also crucial to maintain the lifestyle we are living and also to upgrade to a better one.

I look at so many of my friends and associates working hard to keep up a lifestyle for their families. They make money by working hard, but they miss out an opportunity of enjoying any of those luxuries with their family because they are just too busy working hard. Soon, work becomes an addiction for them and they can't think of doing anything else.

There are people who cannot take a vacation, but not because they can't afford one - for them, there is a feeling of guilt over taking a vacation, as they are obsessed with a pseudo-sense of productivity. Their life becomes so robotic that getting free time drives them crazy. Even when they get some free time they may fill it with unimportant work. They are scared that if they stay calm, some of the suppressed hardcore issues may pop up and stare them in the face, which may not be too comfortable to address.

I call it the prosperity trap. One is trapped by the very prosperity one is seeking to improve one's life. So an optimum lifestyle is one that gives you the freedom, both financially and in terms of time, to pursue the things in life that that you truly value.

## PURPOSE

There is one question that can change the direction of your life and help you discover not only where you wish to go but also why you wish to get there; and that is, "What is the purpose of your life?" It is a very crucial question one must ask oneself and seek an answer. Many people spend their whole life without really knowing what the purpose of their existence on this planet is. The answer to the question may not come as easily as something like, "What is your hobby?" Purpose is much deeper and it exists in the form of 'knowing.' Sometimes you just know that you are meant to do certain things. It could be:

- *To travel the world and discover everything that it has to offer.*

- *To help others discover and fulfil their dreams.*

- *To make the city a better, cleaner place for future generations.*

- *To excel in whatever you do.*

- *To live an ethical life and bring ethical values to your industry.*

Your purpose is often linked to your passion. Once you discover that, you feel empowered and your life gains new meaning and becomes an enchanting journey.

To be able to attain your purpose, you need to break it down into achievable goals. Suppose your purpose is to build up a business empire. It is important to write a mission for your business. Where do you wish to take your business, and what goals do you see it achieving?

A strong mission statement is one that is personal and draws on your emotions:

*"The mission of my business is to help people become better individuals, improve their health, and lead happy and prosperous life using _____ products as a vehicle."*

A weak mission statement would be:

*"My mission is to make a lot of money selling* _____ *products."*

It is a weak statement because once you have the money; you will no longer have a mission. Without a mission, there will be no emotions; and without emotions, there will be no relationships. And it will not be long before your business suffers its own death. Once the mission and the purpose are clear, it becomes easier to set goals and work out a plan to accomplish those.

## SUCCESS

Success means different things to different people. The dictionary defines success as 'the accomplishment of an aim or purpose.' It assumes that you already have an aim and a purpose you wish to achieve. Very often, our aim and purpose is defined by society and the environment around us. It is said that if you do what everyone else does, you will get what everyone else gets.

You will find that each person has his own definition of success. What definition works for one person may not work for another. It is a combination of your desires, emotions, feelings, and thoughts. Success is when you discover what you want in life and start moving towards that goal. Very often, we start following someone else's definition of success and then wonder why we are not motivated to achieve. If you are having difficulty moving forward, it is very much possible.

Here are some questions that are useful for a reality check.

Q1. *What are you currently doing in life in terms of your profession?*

Q2. *Is this what you chose to do, or have you chanced upon it and are continuing to work at it for the money?*

Q3. *On a scale of 1 to 10, how happy are you at this moment?*

Q4. *How many hours do you work or put into your business every day?*

Q5. *How many hours do you spend with your family or your friends in a week?*

Q6. *Are you happy with your current lifestyle?*

Q7. *What is that you are looking for? Would you like more time or more money?*

Q8. *Do you think your current profession can give you more time or money, or perhaps both?*

Q9. *If no, then what are you doing currently that will help you make more money and time?*

Q10. *Do you have a dream or a goal in life? More importantly, if you do indeed have a dream, is it really your own dream, or is it somebody else's?*

Q11. *If it is your own dream, then do you think your current profession or lifestyle can help you achieve your dream or your goal?*

Q12. *If no, then what steps have you taken so far to achieve your dreams?*

Q13. *Have you identified what excuses you are holding on to for not growing personally and financially? (My education is insufficient, the markets are bad, I am too old, and so on)*

These questions will stand like a mirror in front of you. The answers to these will reflect the deep-rooted truths. The revelations are your own, and nobody knows you better than yourself. Once you are face-to-face with your own reality, confronting them will initiate the change for better and will raise you to a new pinnacle of success.

## TAKEAWAY

- *Network marketing is a people's business, and if you wish to succeed in this business, it is important to understand the building blocks—people, and what really motivates and inspires them.*

- *When you build lasting and trusting relationships, business happens on its own. So an optimum lifestyle is one that gives you the freedom, both financially and in terms of time, to pursue the things in life that that you truly value.*

- *Without a mission, there will be no emotions; and without emotions, there will be no relationships. And it will not be long before your business suffers its own death.*

- *Success is when you discover what you want in life and start moving towards that goal.*

*Chapter 3*

# WHY SIGN UP?

"Success is not the key to happiness. Happiness is the key to success. If you love what you are doing, you will be successful."

**~ Herman Cain**

Just say the phrase 'network marketing' at a social gathering and you would get different reactions from various people in the group. Some see it as an industry where people make large sums of money quickly, others see it as a way of building a royalty income after putting in a few years of work, while still others have had the unfortunate experience of being made false promises by an overenthusiastic networker and think that this industry is out to get your money.

Amidst all the various opinions, the dignity and richness of this industry often goes unnoticed. Even people who are already in the industry sometimes fall short of describing what it's really all about. The purpose of this book is to dispel the misconceptions about network marketing and show this industry for what it is and how you can get the best from it.

A question often asked is, "Why should one join network marketing?" Well, my reply is, because it is such a good opportunity to meet people, make great friends, and to be an entrepreneur.

## DO YOU QUALIFY?

After studying the lives of various successful people, the one thing I found in common is that they all took an opportunity when it presented itself. Yes, opportunity knocks, but it doesn't put a sofa outside your door and sit there waiting for you. You need to open the door and grab it.

Network marketing is a rewarding business that can grant you more freedom and an ideal lifestyle. It allows you to create a home-based business with several perks such as working independently or within groups of other entrepreneurs like yourself. This business opportunity does not require you to have any special skills or sales abilities, and the products give you large existing market. The elements needed to succeed in this industry are a dream and the willingness to learn.

As you go through this book, you will be introduced to various ways to build your business; but with just these two things in place, I believe that one can make it to the top. A learner is someone who is willing to nurture and practice the things which have been done and achieved by others, and who is able to inculcate these elements in his own life to succeed.

A dream is a desire that you would like to see fulfilled. Every dream starts with a thought, kindles with emotion, and then gets driven with the effort of the individual. Of course, it is important to understand the company you are interested in order to figure out whether it is the right company for you or not.

## WHICH COMPANY IS RIGHT?

There are certain factors that should be explored while choosing a company. It is important to know about the background of the company that you are going to be a part of. You could look out for the following:

- *General reputation of the company - its legal standing and character*
- *Quality of the products*
- *Pricing of the products*
- *Vision of the company*
- *Vocabulary of its distributors*
- *What are they promising? Are they delivering those promises?*
- *Will they be paying you as promised?*
- *What do people say about the person trying to sponsor you?*

It is important to know whether the people in the company you are considering are truly happy or whether they are just pretending to be happy to attract and allure you. Look at the education system it follows. If the system insists on only the best practices, the distributors will stay the course and succeed. If the company cuts corners and makes compromises, there will be lots of failures, giving not only the company but also the industry a bad name. Weeds grow automatically, but flowers have to be planted. Every good practice has to be installed correctly and monitored to work right.

## SURVIVAL OF THE FITTEST

In a traditional job you are trading hours for currency. So the more hours you spend, the more money you make. But there is a limit to that, because you have only twenty-four hours a day. Most people adjust their wants to their income.

Then there are people who want to make it big as entrepreneurs. To realize this dream they start a business. Unfortunately, the statistics don't look too good. They say that the success ratio for new start-ups in business is 1:100. Of a hundred entrepreneurial ideas that take off, only one goes on to become a business. Now, the ratio for surviving businesses is 1:10. That means only 10% of businesses that make it actually survive in the real world. For a successful entrepreneurial start-up, here are a few things you would need at hand:

- *A feasible business idea*
- *Funds—for infrastructure, salaries, software, technology, etc.*
- *Technical skills for the industry you have chosen*
- *Logistics—a supply chain*
- *Manpower to handle everything - a team. Sales, admin, accounts, operations*
- *Financial knowledge—an accounts department to handle taxation and financial matters*
- *An auditor—to check on financial errors*
- *A consultant—for technical, legal and unpredictable issues*
- *Marketing—to an ever-changing environment*

After having all of these, the survival chances of your business could be only 10%. Doesn't sound like a very exciting proposition, right?

Unfortunately, there is no utopia where the government, laws, and social conditions are all perfect. It's a dynamic environment with constantly changing laws, regulations, trends, and everything. This benefit of network marketing is that although you own your business, all the legal hassles, accounting problems and taxation, analyses of trends, quality control, investment in software, technology and so on are all taken care of by the company. You just use your networking skills to go financially free.

I remember meeting a young man who came up to me at a function and said, "Thank you for bringing meaning to my life." We all like someone who acknowledges our contribution. As I started chatting with him to find out what brought about this gratitude, the story that emerged was an interesting one.

The young lad had signed up because he wanted financial freedom. He was already an entrepreneur with a business selling electrical materials, but was unhappy with the financial returns as well as his lifestyle, because he worked 72 hours a week and did paperwork on Sundays. He liked the thought of having a side income and meeting new people.

Initially, he gave very little time to building his network, because he was still 'stuck' in his conventional business. But he had made a firm determination to meet 5 prospects a week, which he followed with utmost discipline. Soon enough, his business was steadily growing in network marketing and the cheques were getting bigger.

But what truly kept him going was the friends he made here and the books and lectures he was exposed to. What dawned on him were the changes he was noticing in his life apart from the cheques, after he started network marketing. He had a strained relationship at home, which had turned around and had become more warm and cordial. His friends told him he was turning from a relatively serious fellow into someone they liked to be around.

From being an introverted person, he was becoming more likeable and attracted people to him naturally. He understood people better and did not confuse objections with rejections. He cared for making a positive change. He liked that about himself. He had found direction.

I smiled at the young man and said, "You are welcome, but the credit goes to you. Did everyone who joined with you get the same benefits? It is about following the path as listed. Most people don't take the medicine but want it to work because the doctor is famous."

We both had a good laugh. What had worked for him was the education system, which most network marketing companies offer. The books, audios, conferences, and meetings had changed his perspective, and interacting with positive people did the rest. People join this business for different reasons. Some enter it because they want their own business and would like to be their own boss. For others, it's the desire for financial freedom that prompts them to join, and still others because they want more time. Some love the personal growth and leadership associated with the systems, others do it because they like the social aspect of meeting people and making friends. Network marketing offers all these and more. You have to find your own WHY, your own reason to join and help others find theirs.

Once, while visiting China, I came across a lady who was a multimillionaire. And she joined the network marketing business. It didn't make sense to the people around her. She already had in her backyard what most people dreamed of achieving. What could she possibly get from network marketing? What could she expect to get from this business?

What they didn't realize, but what she did, was the joy of helping other people achieve their dreams, which gave her life more meaning and purpose. She chose to count her success by counting how many people were better off because she existed. It is a great feeling when you set another person on a path to financial freedom. And the only high better than tasting success, is when you can help others to taste it.

So this is a business of sharing. Somebody once heard me say this at a lecture and said, "That all sounds good in the books, but aren't all of us selfish? We want to help ourselves first. 'I' want to be a millionaire. I don't care about others."

Well, my answer is this: "Success in this industry is dependent on helping others succeed. There are tools and techniques available to build the business for yourself. But your success would be short-lived and you would not benefit from all the goodness the industry has to offer - which is why you signed up in the first place."

What we are presenting here is a way of earning millions while keeping your ethics, sanctity, and soul intact. Why? Because this is the only business where you grow out of the blessings and goodwill of other people. You are constantly dealing with imperfection in the world—with people, with processes, and with products. Your house, your spouse, your car, your job, nothing would be perfect. Likewise, the people in this business also may not be perfect. What you want is the best to stay with you.

One principle is that whatever you focus upon starts to grow. I have a large collection of business books with titles like 'The Secret of X,' 'What You Always Wanted To Know About Y,' and 'What They Don't Teach You at Z.' All their methods are secrets. I thought I would write a book called 'Secrets of Network Marketing,' but unfortunately there are no secrets here. This is one industry where your leaders should share with you all the methods needed for success, and also help you to copy it to perfect duplication—there are no patents, no copyrights on success in the amazing world of network marketing.

## TAKEAWAY

- *To answer the question, "Why should one join network marketing?" my reply would be, because it is such a good opportunity to meet people, make great friends, and to be an entrepreneur.*

- *Network marketing is a rewarding business that can grant you more freedom and an ideal lifestyle. It allows you to create a home-based business with several perks such as working independently or within groups of other entrepreneurs like yourself.*

- *The elements needed to succeed in this industry are a dream and the willingness to learn.*

- *This is the only business where you grow out of the blessings and goodwill of other people.*

- *It is a great feeling when you set another person on a path to financial freedom, and the only high better than tasting success is when you can help others taste it.*

*Chapter 4*

# LIVE YOUR DREAMS

"Champions aren't made in gyms. Champions are made from something they have deep inside them – a desire, a dream, a vision. They have to have the skill, and the will. But the will must be stronger than the skill."

**~ Muhammad Ali**

There is an interesting story I came across a few days back. It is about a woman who dreams every night that she is being chased around a big haunted house by a huge monster. Night after night, this hideous creature runs after her, with its breath like acid running down the back of her neck. She is terrified when the monster comes near her. The haunted house and the scary gigantic creature seem to be so real.

The woman is so petrified by this dream that she is on the verge of losing her sanity. Finally, one night, the dream begins again, but this time it is different. The beast who had been chasing her till then corners the poor woman, and just as it's about to tear her apart, the woman finds her voice and shrieks, "What are you?! Why are you chasing me? What will you do to me?"

At that, the monster stops, straightens up, and with a puzzled expression, puts its hands on its hips and says, "How should I know? It's your dream."

It is indeed our dream and we can choose to create monsters, or we can choose to create happiness and prosperity.

We all have dreams. As children we have a dream to own a favourite toy, or to go to a favourite restaurant, or to become a famous player or a musician. As we grow up, the nature of our dreams changes to owning a car or a house, going for a dream holiday, or having a fantastic career. In fact, we never stop dreaming. We are dreaming even during our waking hours.

The real challenge is fulfilling these dreams. Do we really work towards our dreams? Do we take a step each day that takes us closer to our dreams? The irony is that in reality, for most people it only remains a dream. Most people's workday is focused on fulfilling the dreams of others rather than those of themselves. Maybe they believe other people's dreams more than that of themselves. Possibly when it comes to following their own dreams they have self-doubts or fear.

I firmly believe that every person is born with a purpose to achieve something in their lifetime. For someone it may be as big as landing on the Moon, for someone else it may be just a vacation on a cruise liner. Both are equally important and may seem equally distant for the respective individuals. People can spend their whole lifetime without really knowing their purpose. Our dreams in life can very well lead us to finding the purpose of our life. Once that is achieved, our life can be really fulfilling.

## DREAMS AND GOALS

A dream is something that is related to feelings and emotions which in turn are driven by the heart; whereas goals are driven by logic and are a function of the mind. If you apply a time frame to your dream, it becomes a goal; and a goal is always easy to achieve.

## PURSUE YOUR DREAMS WHOLEHEARTEDLY

Having clarity about dreams is of utmost importance. The people who have achieved something in their lives are very clear about their dreams and their purpose. Many people are living other people's dreams, knowingly or unknowingly. "My dad wanted me to become a doctor," or "My teacher says I should be pursuing literature," are commonly heard statements. But this is what other people think about you; so they are other people's dreams, not yours. As Steve Jobs very famously said, "Your time is limited, so don't waste it living someone else's life. Don't be trapped by dogma - which is living with the results of other people's thinking. Don't let the noise of others' opinions drown out your own inner voice. And most important, have the courage to follow your heart and intuition."

## EVERY DREAM COMES WITH A PRICE

I remember back in college a friend of mine introduced me to someone he knew who was a bodybuilder. When I met him, I was in complete awe of him. He had a well-chiselled body that was in fantastic shape. I looked at him and said, "Wow, I would love to have a body like yours."

He looked at me straight in the eyes and said, "Of course you can have it - but are you willing to pay the price?" I was confused.

He continued, "I eat eight raw eggs first thing in the morning before I go out for a one hour run, and then I spend three hours at the gym, broken into two slots. I eat boiled chicken breast with no rice or bread for lunch. I carry my own lunch to work and rarely cheat on my diet."

That was his dream - to get a perfect body and participate and win in bodybuilding competitions. He was willing to pay the price. Nobody had to wake him up to tell him to go run, nobody had to push him to go to the gym, and his mother never had to stop him from eating junk food.

## RECOGNIZE AND DECODE YOUR DREAMS

They say that even eagles need a push. In our case, this job is usually done by close friends and family. But this can be done to a certain extent, after which we need to take it forward. But if someone is pushing you hard and you are not really interested, be assured that they are trying to live their dreams through you.

There are a few signs to recognize the ownership of your dreams. Ask yourselves the following questions:

"Does it give you goose-bumps when you think of it?"

"Is there a twinkle in your eyes when you speak of it?"

"Are you all charged up while talking about it?"

Let's say you have a dream of owning a mansion. You put up a picture of your dream house overlooking the sea, with French windows and a gallery with a vine growing on the railing. Do you feel like putting your feet on that balcony and feel the wind in your face? When you see the picture, does it make you miss a heartbeat or make your heart flutter? If it doesn't, it's probably not your own dream.

What do you imagine when you see your dream house? The hurdles, or the opportunities? Sometimes, even when we are all charged up, a little monster in our head does a little moral policing and says, "Hello, but this is not for you. How could do you even think that you would ever own this?" This is dangerous, because when faced with hurdles, you won't be able to overcome them easily. But a person who owns his dream will find the hurdle not an obstacle, but an opportunity.

Another litmus test is this. When you are back, tired from a hard day's work, do you still feel like looking at your dream board? Does it make you feel energized looking at it? Or when you look at it, does it reminds you of what you cannot achieve? If the dream charges you up, excites you, and motivates you to an extent that you feel a surge of energy and you feel like lifting yourself up and reaching for it - it is all yours!

Say your best friend speaks passionately about a specific car model which is his dream. Soon enough, you also want one and think it's your dream to own that car. But when you pause and look deeper, your own dream is to probably travel the world. So at one point you 'bought' his dream and adopted it instead of your own.

Get specific and go into the details of the image you hold in your mind. For example, if your dream is to send your son to a particular college, let your imagination paint a vivid picture of that college. Go visit the college and make it real to your mind. Visualize walking with him on the campus on the first day of college, visualize the happy expression on his face, visualize yourself appreciating him for his excellent performance in class. Go a step further - visualize his graduation and celebrating his success. Now that adds emotion and realism into your dream. Half-hearted dreams are only wishful thinking. There is no better way of showing ownership and focus towards your dreams than by feeling them today and living them tomorrow.

## HAVE THE COURAGE TO DREAM

When asked about their dreams and goals, most people would promptly hand you a 'wish list.' A dream is not to be confused with a wish. A dream is connected to your passion. It is deep-rooted. A wish is something you desire, but you are not willing to pay the price and get it 'come what may.' Sometimes we don't have the courage to dream big. And because of the lack courage to dream big, we fall short of the energy to follow our dream through. One of the reasons we are scared to dream big is because there have been so many don'ts thrown at us right from childhood:

"Don't do that."

"Don't run so fast, you will fall."

"Don't climb that high."

"Don't try that."

And so on, until we withdraw from our own ability almost to the point of denial.

When you have a big dream, there are times when people around may not really understand it. You may want to own a Ferrari, or have an island in the south of France, or become an entrepreneur. Well, people might ridicule that dream, so you should be very careful to share it only with people who would support you. Share it with the world only when you are able to achieve it. The only thing that can really stop you from reaching your dreams is you.

So take a few steps to take ownership of your own dreams:

## BREAK DOWN YOUR DREAM INTO ACHIEVABLE GOALS

Dreams need to be converted into achievable goals. Start with writing down your dream and giving it a deadline. If the dream is big and you find it difficult to relate to, you may need to go through several smaller achievable goals first. If you want to climb Mount Everest, plan on getting to the base camp to start with.

## TAKE ACTION

The law of attraction works best when followed up with the law of action. Just having a dream is no good. Give it a deadline and it becomes a goal. The next step is to move closer to it and to do something to get you closer; and that involves action! Take a step or two towards your dream each day. Enjoy the process. The journey needs to be as much fun as the destination.

## LOOK AT YOUR DREAMS DAILY

We often hear children say they want to become a pilot or an astronaut or a scientist; only to find them sitting behind a desk, cursing their job, fifteen years later. What went wrong? They lost sight of their dream. Either people told them it was not possible, or they got caught up in the cycle of meeting various expectations that other people had of them.

What dreams did you have as a child? Put up pictures around you that remind you of your dream and look at them every day.

## GUARD YOUR DREAMS

There are a lot of people out there who will ridicule you and make your feel small and stupid for having your dreams. Generally, I have noticed that these are people with no dreams of their own who are jealous of the fact that you even have one. Sometimes these 'dream stealers' could also be people close to you, who do it unconsciously or unintentionally. So it is very important to guard your dreams.

Where you stand today is a reflection of your dreams and what you believe you deserve; and your belief is what defines your possibilities.

## TAKEAWAY

- *If you apply a time frame to your dream, it becomes a goal; and a goal is always easy to achieve.*

- *Our dreams in life can very well lead us to finding the purpose of our life. Once that is achieved, our life can be really fulfilling.*

- *Many people are living other people's dreams, knowingly or unknowingly.*

- *There is no better way of showing ownership and focus towards your dreams than by feeling them today and living them tomorrow.*

- *The law of attraction works best when followed up with the law of action.*

- *The only thing that can really stop you from reaching your dreams is you.*

*Chapter 5*

# PROSPECTING

"A single question can be more influential than a
thousand statements."

**~ Bo Bennett**


Any business, big or small, irrespective of its
nature, is based on relationships. There are a minimum
of two people are involved: a 'giver' and a 'taker,' or
a 'seller' and a 'customer.' This is independent of the
nature of the business or whether it is a commodity
trading or a service provided.

Network marketing, as the name suggests, is all
about networking and relationships. Being a business
of its kind, it has some unique terminologies. In
network marketing, the term 'prospect' is a short-
form used for 'prospective customer.' The next
question that arises is, "Who is the prospective
customer?" Well, the answer is 'everybody.' Anyone
could be your next prospect - the person sitting next
to you in a train or plane, someone you accidentally
meet at a party, or even somebody very close to you,
like a relative or a friend.

There is another term known as the 'suspect.'
You may get a 'lead' or information about someone
who might be interested in your business and your
products. This person is a suspect who possibly could
turn into a prospect. They need to qualify to be a

prospect before you can invite them to see the plan and present them a business opportunity.

I like to correlate prospecting to diamond mining. Just as the deeper you dig in a mine, the better your chances of finding diamonds are; similarly, the more people you network with, the better are your chances of finding the right prospects who will shine in your group. This way you invite a better possibility of getting quality prospects.

However, prospecting is much more than only finding the right prospect, writing to them, calling them up, or meeting with them. There is a deeper question which holds the key to true prospecting: do you actually care about the prospect? Or do you want him to buy something off of you, just so that you can make some money? If your answer is the first, it will be much easier for you to grow your network.

After a while, you start developing an instinct that lets you tell who would sign up and who wouldn't. However, just like the diamond mining example, after a while it boils down to statistics - the further down you dig, the greater your chances are of getting more diamonds; similarly, the more people you prospect, the higher are your chances of conversion and growth.

Let's take a look at the nuts and bolts of prospecting.

## QUALIFYING

An important rule to prospecting is not to pass judgement. Just because you think a person is a good fit does not mean he is one. There are times where a person you feel is quite an unlikely candidate for the business goes on to build your biggest group. Meeting people is critical to qualifying. You may wish to ask a few questions to check if the person qualifies as a prospect, such as, "Are you happy with your life in terms of time and money?" or "What are your dreams?" or "Do you have dreams that you see your current career is not fulfilling?"

Find out if that person has a spark and is serious about his answers to your questions. Where there is a spark, you can fan it into a flame with the help of your upline and the system.

When meeting with suspects, you will come across two broad categories of people:

- *People who are ambitious and are looking for something in life*

- *People who have lost the courage to dream.*

The first category is always up to take opportunities and just needs to be shown one. The second category, however, will take a little longer to join in. It does not mean that you should write them off. You will find some really talented people in this group who have stopped believing in themselves due to their circumstances. The trick is to help them rediscover their dreams and help them see why they should join this business and use it as a vehicle to achieve those dreams.

Once you do this, you can see a drastic change in the person. A person who was initially uninterested changes to a self-motivated and passionate person ready to build the network.

## EXPLORE THE MINDSET

While qualifying, explore the mindset of the prospect. Gauge for yourself how far he is open to making an investment for his dream or earning an additional income. Furthermore, find out whether the person is keen to learn and earn. If you feel the person has a completely closed mind, then showing them the plan will be a waste of your time and energy.

If you have a good offer to make, you don't need to over-sell it. So qualify your prospects before getting into showing them the plan. But to qualify people, you need to interact with them. Find out how they respond, whether they have dreams and ambitions, fears, and insecurities, and so on. And if they do, you just have the vehicle for them.

## MAKING A LIST

Very often while making a list, out of all the people you know, you may include some, while ignore others who don't match up to your expectations. But the most important thing to remember here is that it is a business list. A word of caution: don't prejudge people. You never know who is looking for an opportunity at what stage in life. So, the first step is to write down as many people as possible in your list. Make sure it consists of at least 500 names. Then pull out all the names on your cell phone and your business card holders. Try for at least 300 people who are not just strangers on your social network but people you have met. Writing a list of contacts is critical to succeeding in network marketing.

# THE ABC OF MAKING A LIST

Once you have a list, make sure you begin sorting it out. By that, I mean putting each individual's name under List A, B or C.

## List A (close friends)

People under List A are those whom you know on a very personal level and share a good rapport with. These are people who would trust you and sign up with you immediately or would be willing to attend the plan without a fuss. They include your family and close friends. You want them to be right up in your downlines, because they are the ones who will benefit the most once you get going.

Since these people are close to you, you know what motivates them. Educate them. Give them the complete know-how of this business and how it will become a vehicle to fulfil their dreams; be it attaining financial freedom, having more time on hand, or getting to meet more and more people. You already know what they would want most and which examples will work with them. Stick to the basics and talk about the positive aspects of the business.

An important thing to keep in mind is that many people who fall in this category would be willing to sign up for their love, respect, or bonding with you. However, that is not the right reason to make them sign up. It's short-term thinking, because it won't last. Rather, have them find their own reasons for signing up, based on their personal goals and beliefs. Show them examples of people who have succeeded in network marketing from their own profession. This will help them relate to the business. Only then will they will grow, and so will you.

## List B (associates)

List B generally features those who are known to you but are not intimate or close to you. These might be your colleagues or casual friends. It would include people you meet on your daily morning walks, in the gym, club house, or building complex, or distant relatives you meet at various family occasions. One tip - do make a proper distinction between List A and B because your approach towards the two will be different. Generally, this tends to be the widest list when you start out.

## List C (strangers – referrals)

These are people whom you do not know directly but know through someone else by 'referral,' or members of your local community or school alumni from another batch. It could also be contacts that are formed while you met someone randomly at a restaurant or bar, or standing in the queue for your favorite movie. The ability to break the ice - speak to a person not known to you, find a common reality, and share your opportunity with that person - allows you to make exceedingly large networks. Be helpful and kind to people. Hold the door for someone, or help another person with their baggage. Once you help people with your heart and give joyfully, you will invariably find yourself building friendships and networks easily.

Many years ago, I was travelling through Taiwan on a project of establishing an education system in South East Asia. I remember boarding a train to go for one of the meetings. There was a couple seated on the opposite seat, who were in their mid-twenties, constantly chatting with each other in Taiwanese. I didn't understand a word, but we exchanged smiles and I pulled out a book to read.

After a while they plucked out something from their bag, which seemed like sweets made out of preserved dried fruits. As they spoke, laughed, and shared the sweets, the lady offered the packet to me and asked in broken English if I would like to try the 'local sweet.' I smiled and took one. It was delicious, and guessing that I liked it looking at my expression, they offered me more, asking me to try 'another flavor.'

The man tried his best to explain me in a language I could understand about the sweets and how his mother-in-law made them by preserving the fruits. This got us chatting and I told them about India, where I came from, and they seemed to be very interested. We shared our reality with each other. They explained to me that they were part of a direct selling company that sold discounted phone cards to make international calls. Cellular phones had just come in back then and it was frightfully expensive to make an international call on one. They gave me the benefits of their cards and by the time we reached the destination, I had called the group I was travelling with and purchased almost a dozen cards from the couple, because everybody in my group wanted one.

By the time I got off the train, I was great friends with the couple and I often used their services in later years whenever I travelled there and recommended them to a number of friends who travelled to the country.

When I think back, what I remember is not two people making a direct sale; only a couple who offered me sweets, who were interested in my country, and who wanted to help me make cheaper phone calls. Do you mind someone speaking to you if they add value to your life? If not, you don't have to be afraid, either; most people like talking to other people.

## KEEP BUILDING YOUR LIST

It's important to keep adding people to your lists regularly. Keep meeting new people and interact with them on a daily basis. Look for leads through your contacts and talk to new people. Once you have a strong database, you have laid the foundation for your business. As in a good restaurant, you won't get far just reading the menu. You've got to select and order to get what you want. So let us move from looking at our wonderful list to contacting and inviting people to explore a world of opportunity.

## A SECRET

Here is a secret that I would like to share with you. List-making is important to succeed in network marketing, as covered in all the points in this chapter, but there is one thing more important. It is the ability to smile at another human being and connect with that person.

Are you able to hold the door for a lady, help someone with their baggage at the airport, or offer a seat to an elderly person? Are you able to connect with people with a sheer desire to help? The secret is that people respond to emotion, and not to technique. If you can keep making friends and keep the friendships alive, if you can be sensitive to others, then you have a lifelong lead-generating machine — yourself.

Not only do the people you help become potential leads, it also makes you feel good as a positive contributor to society. Making lists is not a one-time activity. Connect with people with all the goodness you can muster and your list will never end.

## TAKEAWAY

- *In network marketing, the term 'prospect' is a short form used for 'prospective customer.' The next question that arises is, "Who is the prospective customer?" Well, the answer is 'everybody.'*

- *The trick is to help them rediscover their dreams and help them see why they should join this business and use it as a vehicle to achieve those dreams.*

- *There are times where a person you feel is quite an unlikely candidate for the business goes on to build your biggest group.*

- *Do you mind someone speaking to you if they add value to your life? If not, you don't have to be afraid, either; most people like talking to other people.*

*Chapter 6*

# INVITING

"If you help enough people get everything in life they want, you'll get everything in life you want."

**- Zig Ziglar**

There is a famous Frank Sinatra song that goes like this:

*Love and marriage, love and marriage,*

*Go together like a horse and carriage.*

*You can't have one without the other.*

Once you are in love with someone and you want to spend the rest of your life together, you propose to the girl. Similarly, contacting and inviting also go hand in hand. Once you are convinced that a prospect qualifies, you move to the next step – inviting.

## THE INVITING SCRIPT

To make your inviting foolproof and successful, it is always best to prepare an invitation script, which should be validated by your uplines. This is a script which should be followed by the system, though every network or organisation may have a few modifications based on the culture of the system. Hence, every networker needs to be armed with an in-depth understanding of what to say, how to say it, and when to say it.

## THE FIRST FEW INVITES

When you have just started, it is best to allow your upline to show the plan, to make the invitation call, tell your prospect about the opportunity, arouse curiosity, and confirm the meeting. Keep it short, regardless of which column your prospects fall in.

The first meeting is very crucial. It is observed that people get put off when you cannot explain your point within a short frame of time. So if you lose your prospects, then you may never get them back again. However, once you are confident, you can take over this activity after checking with your upline. When you start inviting people on your own, remember, the intention is to get an appointment with a commitment on the time and place where you are meeting to show the plan. It is very important to remember that you are trying to get an appointment, not get the prospect to sign up over the phone. Be brief, and show the plan only in person.

## DON'T GET CARRIED AWAY

Very often, in our excitement to show the plan, we tend give out so much of unnecessary information that the prospect is overwhelmed with this overload and backs off due to confusion. This often happens when you don't know the person well. So give them some space. When the person arrives, make sure they are comfortable, and allow them to get into the right frame of mind. Help them settle them down. Talk to them about themselves: show interest in their work, their locality, or what matters to them.

## STICK TO THE POSITIVE

How would you like it if someone comes up to you out of the blue and asks you a direct question about your dreams and your income, and then brings to light what's missing in your life? Would you entertain such a person? Well, I surely wouldn't. Don't put off your prospects by telling them what is lacking in their life. No one likes to confront such questions head-on.

Instead, take a real interest in their life. Put a lot of positive and probing questions to them about their life and dreams, and in a fashion which leads to them having a cognition or realization of what is missing in their life. They will come up with the answers. It is important that you overcome the temptation to jump the gun and tell them about the missing things in their life, even if you can see them.

People love what they realize on their own. It brings forth a conviction in them. A person who is told his life is actually a 'prosperity trap' may just go into denial, defend himself, and close himself to whatever you have to offer; whereas a person who realizes this on his own will say, "Hey, this is not the life I want! Let me see what you have to offer."

Listen attentively. Appear present to the prospect and gently direct the conversation to help the person find his answers. This listening will also provide you with a lot of valuable data on the prospect which helps later down the line when he signs up.

## TALK ABOUT LIFESTYLES

Lifestyles today revolve around a number of things, most of which can be broken down into time and money. When discussing a person's lifestyle, you are in a position to show them the benefits of the business. You can talk about how they are trading hours for money and how this is a fantastic opportunity to reach their dreams, and the lifestyle they desire. Many people will discover why they want to join your business while having this discussion itself.

## EXCITEMENT IS CONTAGIOUS

Excitement is contagious. It converts a dull atmosphere into a lively one. It is your business, so you have to be excited about it. The more excitement you show to your prospects, the more curiosity will grow inside them. If your conviction is genuine, it will reflect in your body language, too.

## MAINTAIN POSTURE

This business is all about posture. Just make your prospect feel that he needs this business more than you need him. Stay in control. Always keep your tone of voice extremely professional and affirmative. Avoid being confirmative; meaning, do not promise anything or build his expectations to such a level that he might fall flat on his face later. Be proud about your business and this exciting opportunity. This will instil belief in the mind of your prospect.

Be clear about the fact that the business is simple but requires hard work and based on the returns you get. Also state that at the end of the day, the hard work is worth it. At any point of time, do not lie or exaggerate about the business or what they can get out of it. Being ethical gets the best results in the long run. A disillusioned prospect is not an asset.

## YOU DON'T HAVE THE WHOLE DAY

Although every prospect is important, don't dedicate the entire day for a single prospect. Keep the call brief, yet effective. Your business will be built by the number of plans you show and not by explaining the business. The most valuable part of the prospecting process is your own time - don't take it for granted.

## TAKEAWAY

- *To make your inviting foolproof and successful, it is always best to prepare an invitation script, which should be validated by your uplines.*

- *It is very important to remember that you are trying to get an appointment, not get the prospect to sign up over the phone. Be brief and show the plan only in person.*

- *When the person arrives, make sure they are comfortable, and allow them to get into the right frame of mind.*

- *Listen attentively. Appear present to the prospect and gently direct the conversation to help the person find his answers.*

- *Many people will discover why they want to join your business while having this discussion itself.*

- *Being ethical gets the best results in the long run. A disillusioned prospect is not an asset.*

## Chapter 7

# SHOW THE PLAN

"Which is the best plan? The plan that you have shown. Which is the worst plan? The plan you didn't show."

**~ Author unknown**

Once you have got the prospect's interest and he's ready to see the plan, you've set the ball rolling. The next step, in network marketing parlance, is to show the plan. Every company has its own plan laid out in detail in the form of a brochure, website, or clearly illustrated format; though the terminology and compensation plans may be different for each company. However, one thing is constant: how you present it.

The best way to start is by introducing the industry and the promise it holds to earn a compounding income. Let the initial dialogue clear the misconceptions regarding pyramid schemes and so on. Explain the actual concept of network marketing and the way one can earn compensation on not only the products used by one, but also on everything used and sold by that person's entire downlines. Quoting a few statistics and figures to build the image of the industry also helps.

The next step is to introduce the company. Focus on its size and strength. This not only gives an assurance but also aids in building trust in the mind of the prospect. Since we are living in the internet age, it is wiser to give people a website they can visit to know more. It will save them the time of searching and will give them the information you want them to know. Tell them about the system offered by the company you work with and how it supports the distributors. Let your enthusiasm do the talking. If you believe in the company and its products and are charged up about the same, your enthusiasm is bound to rub off on the prospect. Know your range of products and be prepared to the handle questions asked about them.

## HELP PEOPLE FIND OUT WHY THEY ARE SIGNING UP

Here is the trick. If you really want to build a big business, just build friends. If you can't find friends, work on yourself. Learn to smile. When you smile at someone and he smiles back, that is when you spark a connection. If you feel that the person needs help and that you can offer some, do it. Make an effort to understand that person and build a connection.

Network marketing is a people's business. Believe in their ambitions and know their fears. See if you can genuinely address those. Help them find what they want in their life and how this business can help them reach there.

Once you can communicate to them the why of the business, the next step is to motivate them to use the products, come to meetings, read more about the company and products, and so on. When you have helped them find their own why, then the person will build the business even without your motivation.

## DRESS FOR SUCCESS

Your appearance is an expression of what you are and reflects your self-image, attitude, confidence, and your state of mind. It creates the first impression of you and the business you are representing. Dress smartly like a leader and be professional. You can dress casually if it's a weekend or if you are meeting on a holiday, but make sure you do not dress shabbily or sloppily. People do judge a book by its cover. One would not wish to be part of a company where the person representing that company is unkempt. Simple things like body odor or bad breath can also put off a prospect. Keep high standards of hygiene when presenting a plan.

## MEET AT A CONDUCIVE AMBIENCE

The whole idea is to make your prospect comfortable. The more comfortable and relaxed you are, the more receptive you become. Ensure that the venue you have chosen is airy and open in order to make your prospect comfortable and focused on the plan. Don't put your prospects in a situation where they are restless and dying to get out of the room for a breather, but are sitting there as a mere formality for the presentation.

## CHOOSE THE RIGHT ENVIRONMENT

Do you want to show the plan at a fancy nightclub or lounge? Not a good idea. There your prospect will look more at the crowd and bob his head to the beats of the music rather than look at your upline explaining the plan. Cut distractions as far as possible. So pick a venue where you can find a quiet corner to present the plan. If you are meeting at a restaurant or coffee shop, don't go overboard when ordering food. The last thing you want is the prospect being too busy with the food to bother about listening to the plan.

## BUILD YOUR UPLINE BEFOREHAND

Before your upline or the speaker enters the venue, talk about your experiences with him or her and explain to the prospect as to how they changed your life. Build it up as a meeting that will bring a transformation to your prospect's life. Credibility can make all the difference. The purpose of this is to have your prospect's complete attention when the upline starts to talk and there is a seriousness built up about the opportunity.

For example you can say, "While we wait for the speaker to arrive, let me tell you more about this wonderful person who changed my life completely. He started his career in X multinational company and after spending Y years in the corporate world [it can be any other field too], he began working on this opportunity, which completely turned his life around. He has been on this project for the last Z years and is doing a phenomenal job. He today makes far more than he could have possibly been making at his job, and he enjoys a fantastic lifestyle. He is rich in time, which he shares with people he loves. I think very highly of him. He had the courage to pursue his dream."

## LET YOUR UPLINE TAKE THE LIMELIGHT

Once your upline or presenter steps into the venue for the presentation, make sure he or she calls the shots. What's important for you is to get up from your chair and shake hands warmly with the presenter. This shows professionalism and also exemplifies that you have an excellent rapport and a warm bond with the presenter. These small signs go a long way towards making an impact on the prospect.

Next, once the plan starts, do not utter a word or interrupt the speaker. He knows more than you, so just keep quiet and listen to what he has to show to your prospect. Acknowledge what is being said, either with a gesture or occasional word. If you look distracted, how do you expect the prospect to take your business seriously? Always express your gratitude to your upline and thank him for giving his valuable time for sharing the business plan.

## STAY ENGROSSED

Cell phones can be a big distraction. What you can do is set your phone on silent, and while doing so, suggest the prospect to do the same. Lead by example. Make this mandatory for every plan, as you are discussing serious business, which means attentively listening to what the speaker has to say. Apply the same rule to yourself. A single call can immediately change the mood and receptiveness of a person.

## POSTURE IS IMPORTANT

Posture does not only mean sitting straight. It also means putting your prospect in a frame of mind that he needs the business more than you need him. Create an air of professionalism and don't guarantee anything or allow yourself to be taken for granted just because the prospect has agreed to see the plan. This is important before, during, and after the plan. Always portray a picture to the prospect that he also needs to qualify to get into the business project even though he knows you. This helps in adding credibility to the business or your company. A posture ensures that every word coming out of the presenter's mouth is taken seriously and the rate of objections and questions comes down drastically.

Examples of bad posture versus good posture:

1.  *"Just join this scheme, man, it's easy."*

    *vs.*

    *"We are looking for key people to partner and expand the business, so are you serious about this opportunity?"*

2.  *"Come on, Steve, we're friends, just come once to see the plan."*

    *vs.*

    *"My senior has only two time slots on Tuesday, which one suits you?"*

3.  *"In this business, you can make lots of money. I give you a personal guarantee that you will make lots of money in this industry."*

    *vs.*

    *"I cannot guarantee you anything. Although a lot of people have made a lot of money using this system, it all depends if my senior partner finds you qualified to take up this project. I need to know*

*why you want to take up this project apart from your daily work."*

Always be firm and never make any false promises, which may spoil your association with your prospect.

## GET ALL THE KEY PLAYERS INVOLVED

If your prospect needs to get their spouse or key decision-makers, make sure they are there for the meeting because you do not want the prospect to discuss a half-cooked plan with the decision-makers. Make sure everyone is on the same page and come to a conclusion by the time the plan is over.

## KEEP IT SIMPLE

The problem with many plans is that they get way too technical and into the numbers and graphs. Instead of burdening the prospect with all these technicalities at this stage, find out what he wants in life. Give him examples of other people who have been where he is and how they have benefited. For example, you could share a story of a doctor with a doctor, or share the success story of a builder with another builder. Use examples of people from the industry of the prospect, because the person will relate to them more easily than to you. Then make him see how this business can help in achieving his dreams or aspirations.

## DUPLICATE THE PLAN

The system will generally be a tried-and-tested formula. Your best bet in making an impression on your prospect is to stick to the presentation methods and practices of your uplines. Keep the proper flow of the entire presentation or you'll end up confusing yourself as well as the prospects, leading them into a zone of uncertainty.

## CARRY ALL YOUR MATERIAL

Pen, paper, pads, and charts, get everything along with you to assist your prospect. And most importantly, carry a laptop or some electronic gadget with an internet connection or payment gateway so that if the prospect is impressed and ready to sign up, you can close the deal then and there without giving him a chance to go back and change his decision.

## CLOSING THE PLAN

After showing the plan, get a feedback from the prospect as to what they liked about the business or the company. This is an important exercise for you to do as you are reemphasizing the reason for the prospect to do the business.

## OBJECTION HANDLING

Keep this right for the end and do not let the prospect interject while you show the plan as this will spoil the flow. Now that your prospect has seen the plan, there could be questions raised. The questions will be typical, such as, "I am not into selling," or "I am not sure about these products," and so on.

There is a whole section on handling objections further in this book. In network marketing, most objections are predictable. This is the beauty of being connected with a system of education. You can benefit from all the objections that have been raised in the past and be prepared with your answers. Objections are good for the business in the long run, because you are signing up a person with fewer confusions and a clearer understanding. Also, never confuse objections with rejections - the two are not the same. A person with more objections may, in the long term, turn out to be your best network builder.

## TAKEAWAY

- *If you believe in the company and its products and are charged up about the same, your enthusiasm is bound to rub off on the prospect.*

- *If you really want to build a big business, just build friends.*

- *Create an air of professionalism and don't guarantee anything or allow yourself to be taken for granted just because the prospect has agreed to see the plan.*

- *Instead of burdening the prospect with all these technicalities at this stage, find out what he wants from life.*

- *Your best bet in making an impression on your prospect is to stick to the presentation methods and practices of your uplines.*

- *Objections are good for the business in the long run, because you are signing up a person with fewer confusions and a clearer understanding.*

## Chapter 8

# FOLLOW UP AND FOLLOW THROUGH

"You don't close a sale, you open a relationship if you want to build a long-term, successful enterprise."

**~ Patricia Fripp**

Once you have shown the prospect your plan and have his interest, the next step in the sequence would be to sign him up. It may happen immediately if the prospect is convinced and ready to go for it, but sometimes it may take a few days if the prospect chooses to deliberate on it.

So how long should a prospect take after seeing the plan to make a decision? Is it a week, ten days, or a month? In my opinion, 48 hours would be the optimum. Your chances decrease significantly every day if you delay closing the deal beyond 48 hours. Having the prospect sign up is only the beginning of growing your business.

What is the difference between 'following up' and 'following through?'

If your prospect declines or delays the decision to do business with you, you still have obligations to that person, which requires following up. If they do become your customer, you need to follow through, ensuring that every promise is completely fulfilled.

The next stage of signing up the prospect within 48 hours is crucial. However, it involves two aspects - apprehensions about closing due to the fear of rejection, and the actual rejection because of the deal not going through.

## HANDLING REJECTIONS

What if the prospect rejects your offer?

The ability to handle rejection is useful in every business, as it is in life. Never confuse the rejection of an opportunity to be a personal rejection. Handle it gracefully. It is always good to address the situation and not assume things. Ask the prospects about their opinion on points that did not appeal to them and listen while they speak. It is important that you do not try to argue about their objections. Never impose your view at such times, however correct it may be, as there is a greater chance of it backfiring. Furthermore, this will close all doors for future communications as well. It is important to note that even if your prospects do not approve of the business, they should be given the space to do so.

You are not a salesman, you are a dream builder; so don't try to hard-sell such a great opportunity. On the contrary, keep the same equation with the prospects. Maybe they do not require the business today but might need it tomorrow. And if they do, I'll bet you that you'll be the first one on their list.

An exercise to understand why the rejection by the prospect occurred will not only help you handle the rejection in a positive way, but will also prepare you better for the next one. An objective analysis about the same can be done based on the following points.

- *Was I able to properly communicate the plan to the prospect?*

- *Did I propose a solution before fully exploring their needs?*

- *Did I do my best possible job of asking questions and encouraging them to share their ideas, or did I spend too much time just presenting my ideas and possible solutions?*

- *Did I put relationship over targets while talking to the prospect?*

- *Did I really help them make the best possible decision that is in their best interests?*

- *By behaving respectfully and professionally, have I left the door open for doing business later if their situation changes?*

- *Based on their reasoning for not buying, will the situation change in the future?*

- *Were there any contrary opinions from those around the prospect?*

Taking an analysis of the rejection does help a great deal in reaching for a probable reason for rejection. Rejection always gives an opportunity to learn and develop. Keep the reason in mind, and carry on with a better understanding of the business and a new friend in life.

After the objective analysis, the next step is to follow up with the prospect. It is seen that in many cases you can often turn a 'no' into a 'yes' if you execute the follow-up campaigns properly. If the prospects try to gain more knowledge over time, there are greater chances of them getting into business.

The prospect may already be in a place where he wants to be, or he may not be prepared to take up an opportunity at the present time. One possible way of following up may be saying something like, "Hey Yash, is everything fine? We were supposed to meet and I just wanted to check if everything is okay. The meeting was great and we missed you. Just checking if all is well. I am sure you wanted to be there, but priorities are priorities - it's a fast world. That said, do call me anytime. I just wanted to leave you a message to let you know that I care." Appreciate the person and let him know you care.

Nevertheless, make sure that you have done your bit in terms of:

- *Sharing the business as an opportunity and not as sale of products*

- *Taking the initiative and introducing the prospect not only to the business but also to an opportunity.*

- *Explaining the business as a platform to earn profits together rather than having a motive to earn money for yourself*

- *Developing a bond with your prospect over the course of several conversations meaning right from the first stage of prospecting till showing the plan.*

If you have followed the steps right, you have 'given' something and have already added value to the prospect's life. This understanding will take away the rejection blues.

## TAKE FEEDBACK

When you get back to your prospects after the plan, get some honest feedback about the business. If they like it, ask them what appealed to them most about the business or the company. Let them come up with what they like about the plan. When they have stated what they like, rather than simply agreeing to your preferences, you will find it much easier to close the deal.

## ENCOURAGE MORE QUESTIONS

Once you have explained the basics, stop. Give some leeway to your prospect. Appreciate the fact that the prospect is new to this concept. Allow and encourage questions. The more questions you answer, the better the prospect can understand the business. If the prospect finds another round of meeting with your upline or presenter agreeable, the chance of getting them on board becomes significantly higher. The prospects you should worry about are the ones who don't ask any questions. This could mean that they did not understand the plan and the opportunity this business holds for them, or that they are simply not interested in the business.

If your upline is not physically available, you can do a quick conference call on the phone so that he and you can handle the questions that the prospect has about the business.

As Malcolm Gladwell pointed out in his best-selling book Blink, almost every person has the innate ability to detect authenticity in another person in mere seconds. Equally important, they do it on a subconscious level; without even knowing they are doing so.

If your intentions are pure, your prospects and clients will subconsciously be compelled to want to do business with you. Conversely, if your intentions are to make money and to push people into making buying decisions and/or manipulate them, then no amount of training, psychology, or technology will help you build a long-lasting career in sales.

## TAKEAWAY

- *Never confuse the rejection of an opportunity to be a personal rejection.*

- *Analysis on the rejection does help a great deal reaching to a probable reason for rejection.*

- *It is seen that in many cases you can often turn a 'no' into a 'yes' if you execute the follow-up campaigns properly.*

- *When you get back to your prospects after the plan, get an honest feedback about the business.*

- *If your intentions are pure, prospects and clients will subconsciously be compelled to want to do business with you.*

*Chapter 9*

# HANDLING OBJECTIONS

"Most fears of rejection rest on the desire for approval from other people. Don't base your self-esteem on their opinions."

**~ Harvey Mackay**

Nothing is perfect in this world. Likewise, there cannot be perfect prospecting and inviting. There are bound to be objections. Questions will be raised during the process of dealing with a prospect. It's absolutely normal. When you go out to buy yourself a phone or a gadget, do you blindly pick it up from a store? No, you always ask the salesperson about the pros and cons, or pose many ifs and buts. Your interest gets stimulated with the number of questions you ask, which in turn increases your chances of buying the product. The key is to be tactful and insightful while addressing and answering each and every question. Here are a few ground rules that may come in handy.

## DON'T OVERDO THE CONVINCING

I reiterate that you are an entrepreneur, and not a door-to-door salesman. If someone does not like the product or the business plan, so be it. Be polite and courteous even if your viewpoints do not match. An error that people make is to judge the other person based on their response to the proposal. Accept people unconditionally with a genuine desire to help, and you will find you don't need to convince people. You are in the business of sharing.

## THINK LIKE THE PROSPECT

If you are proactive and talk about the objections of the prospect before he does, it shows that you are thinking like him and he will relate to you. So, if you pose questions and give solutions on the spot, the prospect will respect your words of advice.

## DON'T GET PERSONAL

You and your prospect have discussed a serious business plan. Now the last thing you want is to ruin your personal relations because of a presentation. If your prospect does not take you seriously or even jokes about your taking up this business, well, don't go with the joke, but keep your poise. Never win an argument and lose a friend. Actions speak louder than words. Let your life be an example.

## THE FEEL, FELT AND FOUND FORMULA

The next time someone raises a question, use the feel, felt and found formula, which is to tell your story to your prospect when you initially joined the business. It should be on the lines of, "Look I know how you feel and that's exactly how I felt when I first started the business. However, once I started, I found out the true potential of this business."

Relate to them and they will relate to the business. It is important that you use the products to be able to use this technique. Let's say you are selling soap and the prospect raises an objection that soaps make your skin dry, you can counter the objection rightly only if you are indeed using the soap and can say with conviction that you use it all the time and have experienced no dryness - that is what is good about this soap. And the other person can tell when you are speaking from real experience. Generally, there is a trend to objections and there are some which are common and often encountered.

Given below is a list of questions that will make it easy to handle most of the objections that come your way.

## OBJECTION HANDLING - FAQs

### Q1. I don't believe in these chain and pyramid marketing firms.

"[Name of prospect], we are not into selling any chains, nor do we form pyramids. Secondly, pyramid schemes are banned in a lot of markets. However, our model is network marketing and direct selling where there are actual products or services being rendered to you with a transaction in return."

Next, build the credibility of your company by stating your business model and products you are offering at the moment. State how long your company has been in the business and the number of your customers globally. This will prove what Abraham Lincoln once said: "You can fool all the people some of the time, and some of the people all the time, but you cannot fool all the people all the time."

## Q2. I don't have the money to get into this business.

"Well, that's exactly why I wanted to share this opportunity with you, because as far as I can see, your Plan A in life is not optimum for the goals you desire. So now is the time to think about Plan B. This, my friend, is the Plan B and if you do get going in the business, a day will come when you will not have to think about any other plans. You may not see the results immediately, but as you apply the compounding principle regularly over a period, you will see magic happening." Also try to reinforce the reason of the prospect, which he had stated to you (his why of joining the business) and tell him that his dream is not going to come true with his current job or designation.

## Q3. I don't have time for this.

"That's exactly why I am calling you - to show you an opportunity which will give you all the time you want for yourself. Many of us might have the money but never the time, and I have seen that this business can correct that situation. A rich man is one who has time."

OR

"OK, can I ask you a question? If you continue doing whatever you are doing right now, will you be getting more time to spend with your family or what you'd love to do in the next 5 years?"

OR

"To make time, you have to set aside some time every day. And I am not telling you to put your entire time into the business. All I am asking you to do is to manage your time in a better way, which means putting 15 to 20 hours every week into the business. Now that's not a lot compared to the benefits of financial freedom, is it? Success is about leveraging time of others and becoming successful. The most successful entrepreneurs have done that." [Name a few top entrepreneurs in the world today]

### Q4. I am not into the selling business.

"Guess what, neither are we. I am not here to sell you anything. I am here only for you to make an informed decision, whether you want to continue at what you are doing or if you are really looking to change your life and become an entrepreneur. And entrepreneurs are not selling, they are fulfilling a vision. This is the business of sharing, not selling."

### Q5. How much money are you making?

"Well, did you ask the same question to your boss or colleagues when you joined a company? You joined because you wanted to get associated with the company as it would help you progress in your career. That's exactly what I want to say. Forget about what I am making, and rather think about how much money you can earn or want to earn. Why stop at me? The beauty of this business is that you can make more than your upline, and find him supporting you."

### Q6. How much money can I make?

"It purely depends on your efforts. People who are successful have already earned millions, but there are also people who have not yet opened their accounts. It all depends on how much effort you are willing to put into the business."

## Q7. This isn't for me.

"What is not for you - the fact that you can dream or that you can become an entrepreneur? Let me put this question to you: don't you deserve more than what you're earning in life right now? If your answer is yes, then this business is definitely for you."

## Q8. I know all about it, it doesn't work.

"Well, it is working for approximately 100 million users worldwide and it is more than a $150 billion industry according to figures from the Direct Selling Association. Now it is up to you whether to make an excuse or make it work for you. This industry has produced more millionaires than any other business or profession in recent times. Well, it surely works. The question is whether you want to work."

You can also tell the prospect that it has worked for you and that you researched and analysed the company before signing up. While telling him about how you cleared your doubts, you just might clear many of his.

## Q9. I need time to think about it.

"Sure. I understand you need time, but remember that the biggest cost in this business is the cost of delay. This means seeing your family and friends being a part of this business through someone else rather than you. A delayed decision equals delayed earnings, it's a simple equation. If you want to try out a few products, I can provide you with samples. Do let me know in a couple of days about the products and your decision."

## Q10. Why are the products overpriced?

"Let me put it another way. If you were to open your business today, how much it would cost you? Now compare it to this opportunity at hand where you are getting a chance to be an entrepreneur at a much lesser cost compared to a traditional business or enterprise."

## Q11. I am busy right now, can I reply later?

"It's not something I can promise you because we are looking to form a team in the next two weeks. If you cannot commit now and if money is not a priority for you at the moment, then let me know sometime in the future when you do have the time. Call me if you are interested, and if there is still a spot for you available then we'll take it from there, but I cannot guarantee anything."

## Q12. I don't want to take more time away from my family.

"That's why I am building this business, so that eventually I get quality family time."

OR

"Let me ask you this, do you want to spend a few weekends with your kids, or would you like to spend a lifetime with them, regardless of whether it is a weekday or a weekend?"

OR

"I don't want to be stuck in a situation where I give my work and my boss more time than my family, that's why I chose this business - to be more with my family than with my boss."

## Q13. Do I have to spend my evenings towards my project?

"This business is completely flexible. It depends on how much time you can spare. The more time you put in, the better the returns."

## Q14. I do not fit into your system.

"Well, if you didn't, why do you think we called you? Trust me, you'd be great at this. You have the perfect credentials for this business."

## TAKEAWAY

- *Your interest gets stimulated with the number of questions you ask, which in turn increases your chances of buying the product.*

- *Accept people unconditionally with a genuine desire to help, and you will find that you don't need to convince people.*

- *Remember, you are in the business of sharing.*

- *If you are proactive and talk about the objections of the prospect before he does, it shows that you are thinking like him and he will relate to you.*

- *Never win an argument and lose a friend.*

*Chapter 10*

# THE COMPOUNDING PRINCIPLE

*"You will never change your life until you change something you do daily. The secret of your success is found in your daily routine."*
**~ Darren Hardy**

Let us take a look at Steve's story. Steve is a gentleman in his mid-thirties. He is working in a company as a manager. His routine for the day is set.

In the morning: Wake up unwillingly with a roaring alarm at 6 a.m., read the newspaper, get ready, hurriedly gulp down some coffee and breakfast, rush to the office while driving through crazy traffic, be barely able to reach the office on time, and stay glued to the computer in the office till the day's work gets done.

In the evening: Start back for home at 8 p.m., go through the same ordeal while driving back, reach home by 9.30 p.m., take a shower, have dinner, watch TV for a while, and go to sleep.

The result: This kind of routine leaves Steve physically exhausted and mentally drained. By the time he reaches home, his children are asleep so he hardly gets to meet them, and his wife is frustrated as he has no time for the family. This leads to arguments between them. His social life is zero. This routine leaves him no time for himself. Finally, he goes to sleep, dissatisfied with how the day was spent and dreading to face the next day. He realizes that his life is completely messed up. In his mind, he screams, "Why can't we have more than 24 hours in a day?"

Do you resonate with Steve's story? Like Steve, I am sure that this thought must have crossed your mind several times: "What if the day was longer than 24 hours? I could earn more money, I could spend more time with my family and friends, and I could invest time in my hobbies. Why do I have to work for money? Can't money work for me?"

The fact is that there are only 24 hours in a day; no matter how talented you are or how much money you get paid for every hour that you work.

But what if I tell you that you can have more time and money within the limited 24 hours in a day? This is possible through the concept of the power of compounding and the principle of leveraging, and network marketing is based on this concept.

You cannot begin to realize the power of these principles until you see them in action. You can see to some extent the power of compounding even in your day-to-day life when you keep doing something, however big or small, consistently over a period of time. The amount multiplies with each effort and over a period you see extraordinary returns.

# THE COMPOUNDING PRINCIPLE

The word compounding refers to the ability of an asset to generate 'earnings' (interest) that are then reinvested to generate their 'own' earnings over and over. In network marketing, your principle is your effort to enrol your new member. When the game of compounding starts and your one new member multiplies into a group, you earn not only due to your effort but also due to the efforts of each one of your team members.

### Scenario 1 – The super salary

Imagine that you were offered Rs. 1 crore a day for a month. That is a fantastic salary, resulting in Rs. 31 crore transferred straight into your bank at the end of the month.

## Scenario 2 – The compounding principle

Now let's look at another scenario, where I hand you Re. 1 on the first day of the month and double the salary each day for every day of the month. How much will be your total income? Not much, right? Maybe scenario 1 was better, correct? Wrong. Did you know that if your income doubles for 31 days, you will end up with more than Rs. 107 crores! How? That is the power of compounding.

To show you how it works, I have used the popular example of the penny which doubles each day of the month for 30 days. It is a classic example in the world of network marketing. Pay attention to the figures to see how the power of compounding works with each passing day.

| DAY | VALUE (in US $) |
|-----|----------------|
| 1 | 0.01 |
| 2 | 0.02 |
| 3 | 0.04 |
| 4 | 0.08 |
| 5 | 0.16 |
| 6 | 0.32 |
| 7 | 0.64 |
| 8 | 1.28 |
| 9 | 2.56 |
| 10 | 5.12 |
| 11 | 10.24 |
| 12 | 20.48 |
| 13 | 40.96 |
| 14 | 81.92 |
| 15 | 163.84 |
| 16 | 324.68 |
| 17 | 655.36 |
| 18 | 1,310.72 |
| 19 | 2,621.44 |
| 20 | 5,242.88 |
| 21 | 10,485.76 |
| 22 | 20,971.52 |
| 23 | 41.943.04 |
| 24 | 83,886.08 |
| 25 | 167.772.16 |
| 26 | 335,544.32 |
| 27 | 671,088.64 |
| 28 | 1,342,177.28 |
| 29 | 2,684,354.56 |
| 30 | 5,368,709.12 |

Now is this the power of the compounding effect. Obviously, if you see what's in your hand after ten days, it is only $5.12 and if you look after 15 days, it's still only $163.84. The real power of the compounding principle becomes visible only as it continues over time every day. The mistake that a lot of new people in network marketing make is that they judge the returns based on the income from the initial days, when the compounding returns seem comparatively low as seen from the chart above. The trick is to get through the initial stage. You can see this concept work in all areas of your life. Try going to the gym and look at your body after a week. Do you see a marked difference?

Now put in an hour every day for a year and look at your body. The effort you put in yesterday is compounding with the effort you put in today. If you were to judge the gains of the first week and make a decision to continue working out, you are not going to sign up for the gym.

## PRINCIPLE OF LEVERAGING

In the network marketing industry, through the power of leverage, you can be compensated on the 'efforts' of hundreds or thousands of people.

The concept of leveraging works in your favor with a similar result. So you start off as a network marketer. No office politics and no boss telling you to stay in late. Now you are working for 20 hours a week and you recruit 3 people. The 3 people you recruited are duplicating your effort and also start working at just 20 hours a week. So your combined total is now 20 + 60 = 80 hours a week. Now each of those 3 people recruit 3 more people the next week. You now have 20 + 60 + 180 = 260 hours of work happening the next week. Who said you only have 24 hours a day, or that you can only work 72 hours a week?

Says John D. Rockefeller, "I'd rather have 1 percent of the efforts of 100 people, than 100 percent of my own efforts." If you sign up just one new prospect into your business every month and you teach that new person to do just the same and the process continued, you would have over 4,000 people within your network by the end of the first year.

When you work for someone else in a traditional job, you only get paid for your own effort. But, in the network marketing industry, with the powerful concept of leveraging, you get compensation on the efforts of tens, hundreds, or even thousands of people, all contributing to your financial success. You could be out on vacation, or spending time with your family, and your bank account is would still be growing, thanks to your network working for you even in your absence. And the beauty of it is that they are chasing their own dreams, which are contributing to yours.

The principles of compounding and leveraging are fool-proof. The challenge is to have focus and be patient till the critical mass is reached. Once that is achieved, your network becomes self-perpetuating. It will grow on its own.

A single pine tree grows hundreds of cones, each with dozens of seeds. Potentially, a single tree could produce an entire forest if each seed was allowed to germinate. So nature also uses the compounding principle to multiply.

Compounding becomes very fascinating as it continues to grow. The majority of the people quit in the initial stages without experiencing the power of this principle at work. But if you work smart and apply this principle to your advantage — well, the sky's the limit.

You can work hard or work smart. The choice lies with you.

## TAKEAWAY

- *Network marketing is based on the principle of compounding and the principle of leveraging.*

- *You cannot begin to realize the power of these principles until you see them in action.*

- *When the game of compounding starts and your one new member multiplies into a group, you earn not only due to your effort but also due to the efforts of each one of your team members.*

- *In the network marketing industry, with the powerful concept of leveraging, you get compensation on the efforts of tens, hundreds or even thousands of people, all contributing to your financial success.*

- *Compounding becomes very fascinating if allowed to continue and it will take your wealth to unlimited levels.*

- *If you understand the principle of compounding, you will never give up.*

## Chapter 11

# BELIEVE AND ACHIEVE

"Whatever the mind can conceive and believe, it
can achieve."

### ~ Napoleon Hill

Since the ancient Greeks and Romans, athletes
from across the world had been trying to break the
record of running a mile in under 4 minutes, but
nobody had broken the 4 minute record – ever. All
sorts of experiments and training had been tried to
achieve this feat, but people believed that the human
body was just not meant to go at that speed. It was
not to be.

But in the year 1954, a 25-year-old British medical
student, Roger Bannister, became the first person in
history to break the record of running a mile in less
than 4 minutes. As part of his training, he constantly
visualized breaking the record, in order to create a
sense of certainty in his mind and body.

Now comes the interesting part. Over the next
few years, a number of runners broke the 4 minute
mile record, and now it is a very common thing
for people to run a mile under 4 minutes. So what
changed? It was the belief! When people saw that is
was possible to break the record and that one man

could do it, suddenly it was possible for anyone to do it.

All it took was a belief that IT WAS POSSIBLE!

Imagine what could happen in your life when you break the beliefs holding you back; when you get hold of the monster whispering in your ear, "I don't think you will make it," and you look that monster in the eye and shout back, "I am already making it!"

Find out what the 4 minute miles holding you back are. Change your beliefs and you can change your life. A positive thought is the most important seed in harvesting your dreams. Let us look at some of the steps to adopt a positive approach towards life.

## THE CHANGE STARTS FROM WITHIN

There is only one thing constant in the world, and that is change. I said that as part of a speech once and an attendee later came to me and said, "Isn't that neat? Everything is constantly changing, so I don't need to do anything to bring about change. Things are going to change on me anyway."

That is funny, and true, but what is important is whether you wish to be the cause of the change or be affected by it. When you are the cause, you can make things change in the direction you want them to and have the life you desire. When you are affected by change, you have to accept what is put on your plate and eat it. The choice is yours. If you keep doing what you have always done, then you will keep getting what you have always gotten. If you want a different life, well, the answer is simple: do something different.

## KEEP YOUR FOCUS ON THE DESTINATION

When you have to climb up a mountain, where do you look? Up at the peak, or down at all the rocks that are going to come in your way as you start climbing? If you look at the obstacles, you can never even make a start.

Most people, when you start telling them about an opportunity, will bring your attention to all the rocks in their way:

"I don't have the time."

"I don't have the money."

"I don't have any social skills."

"I don't know any friends who would want to join me for this opportunity."

STOP! This is when you need to help them shift their gaze from the obstacles to the destination. And what's more, you need to be looking at it yourself. THAT is when the obstacles become smaller and you become bigger.

You could have been doing what you do for a very long time, but it's never too late to change. Colonel Sanders was 65 years old when he started Kentucky Fried Chicken (KFC), and Ray Kroc was a milkshake machine salesman at 52 when he decided to start McDonald's. Thomas Edison tried thousands of times before actually succeeding at creating the light bulb.

What was common to each of them was the belief in the destination rather than the potholes on the way. If your destination is to become wealthy as a networker, you need to keep your focus on that top position and on taking your group there with you, not on self-limiting beliefs that will sabotage your success. Identify your doubts and face them early on. It makes the road ahead faster and smoother.

## KEEP POSITIVE COMPANY

Have you noticed how many people take up a class or a form of exercise such as cycling or yoga or going to the gym, and give up after a few days? There are also some people who take up network marketing and give up within a few days or a few months. Same reason – they don't believe it's going to make a difference to their lives. They don't trust themselves to make a difference.

It is said that you can tell a man by the books he reads and the company he keeps. You'll meet people who will downplay both your business and you. These are people who will make you feel smaller than you are and will make you unsure about reaching your goals.

Negative thoughts are like weeds which grow automatically, anywhere. One needs to keep trimming them out. Positive thoughts are like plants - you have to sow them and nurture them, but the effort is worth it.

If you look like a garbage bin, people will come and put trash your way; they will come to gossip with you and discuss how terrible the world conditions are. If you sow seeds of happiness and look like you are on your way to success, people will want to discuss future plans with you and talk about their success. You can CHOOSE!

## TAKEAWAY

- *Change your beliefs and you can change your life.*
- *If you keep doing what you have always done, then you will keep getting what you have always gotten.*
- *Identify your doubts and face them early on, it makes the road ahead faster and smoother.*
- *Positive thoughts are like plants - you have to sow them and nurture them, but the effort is worth it.*

*Chapter 12*

# PERSISTENCE

"The pessimist sees difficulty in every opportunity. The optimist sees the opportunity in every difficulty."

**~ Winston Churchill**

There is a well-known story about two frogs. One frog was fat and the other was skinny. One day, while searching for food, they inadvertently jumped into a vat of milk. They couldn't get out as the sides were too slippery and the vat was deep, so they just kept swimming around. The fat frog said to the skinny frog, "Brother, there's no use paddling any longer. We're just going to drown, so we might as well give up."

The skinny frog replied, "Hold on, brother, keep paddling. There is always hope." And so they continued paddling for hours.

After a while, the fat frog said, "Brother, there's no use. I'm becoming very tired now. I'm just going to stop paddling and drown. We're doomed. There's no possible way out of here." And the fat frog stopped. He gave up. And he drowned in the milk. But the skinny frog kept on paddling. His arms became more and more tired, and it became harder and harder and harder for him to swim.

Despite his limbs aching, he kept trying and trying; it seemed as if the milk was getting hard and heavy. He knew that he would probably die, but as long as he'd got a little bit of life left in him, he was going to keep on swimming. On his last stroke, it seemed as though he had to pull a whole ocean towards him, but he did it, and suddenly felt something solid beneath his feet. He looked around and found himself sitting on a vat of butter. He had churned the milk into butter. He hopped out of the vat, well rewarded for his persistence.

The ability to hold on to or bounce back in life, fighting all odds, working tirelessly despite all failures, is nothing but persistence; and it is our persistence that will determine the outcome of any endeavor that we undertake.

## IT'S ALL ABOUT PERSISTENCE

The evolution of the human race can be summarised in just one word - persistence. If it wasn't for persistence, man would never have progressed. There would be no civilization and we would still be living in the Stone Age. We are today a result of various people's endless persistence and endeavors to improve and advance our lives. Our persistence has paid off. Had Thomas Edison given up on the light bulb after a thousand attempts, we would still be in darkness today. If Mahatma Gandhi had given up his non-violence struggle, India would have not gained independence. Agatha Christie faced several rejection letters from publishers in the first four years of her writing before she got a break, and she went on to be listed in the Guinness Book of Records as the highest selling novelist of all time.

# PERSISTENCE DOES NOT SEE APTITUDE, JUST ATTITUDE

If you set your sights on something, pursue it and never give up. Abraham Lincoln had no formal education but went on to become the US President. Despite losing several elections before, he ultimately succeeded. In network marketing, no matter what walk of life you come from, if you persist and keep a positive attitude, your success ratio automatically goes up because so many fail to even envision their dreams.

# PERSISTENCE IS A SKILL

Have you ever sown a seed and seen it through its growth, developing into a big tree? It is a long process for a seed to blossom into a full-grown tree; sometimes it may take years. You simply cannot push it to grow. It will take its own time to bear fruits. It is a process that requires patience and persistence. It needs to be nurtured for it to transform into a healthy tree. Similarly, when you start any new venture, persistence is the key to see it through. There may be failures, dull moments, self-doubts, and times when you may feel like giving it all up. This is exactly where persistence will help. It is a skill. Some people have it naturally, while others may need to develop it. Nature is a great teacher of persistence. It is quite a sight to see an ant climb a vertical surface. It falls down so many times, but never quits. It will get up the very next moment and start again till it reaches its destination. Even if you put an obstacle in front of the ant, it will change its course, but it will never stop. That is persistence. It is undoubtedly one of the most important ingredients of success.

## STAY IN THE GAME

If you have entered the business with questions lingering in your mind, take a simple piece of advice. Quit right now! This is a demanding business and will test your patience and persistence. When you did not question your boss on the first day of your job about your role in the organization or the problems you might face. Did you have any ifs or buts when you got married? You took a plunge in various things in life with a 'no conditions apply' motto, so why take up the business conditionally? Do it unconditionally, and your earning potential will be unlimited.

## THE BUSINESS WORKS - DO YOU?

It's funny how people question the network marketing industry, its model, and its functioning. In reality, they should be checking how much work they have put into the business. The industry has transformed the fortunes of millions around the world, who in turn have earned millions of dollars from the business. These are people who have remained committed and swore by their dreams despite highs and lows. They persisted and came out on top. The real question is: Are you willing to work in this business and make it work for you?

## IT'S NOT JUST ABOUT YOU

When you follow the rules and get it right, it's easy to reach your dreams. However, even when you do reach your dreams, it's not the end of the journey. By the time you reach your dreams in network marketing, you will have invariably reached a leadership position. Now you have the responsibility of ensuring that your team members also fulfil their individual dreams. Every time you cross a personal milestone or achieve a goal, as a leader you have to take others across the finish line as well. Persistence is the name of the game.

## TAKEAWAY

- *Persistence is nothing but the ability to hold on to or bounce back in life, fighting all odds, and working tirelessly despite all failures.*

- *If you set your sights on something, pursue it and never give up.*

- *There may be failures, dull moments, self-doubts, and times when you may like giving it all up. This is exactly where persistence will help.*

- *This is a demanding business and will test your patience and persistence.*

- *When you follow the rules and get it right, it's easy to reach your dreams. However, even when you do reach your dreams, it's not the end of the journey.*

*Chapter 13*

# ATTITUDE IS EVERYTHING

"Nothing can stop the man with the right mental attitude from achieving his goal; nothing on earth can help the man with the wrong mental attitude."

**~ Thomas Jefferson**

One day, a traveller was walking along a road on his journey from one village to another. As he walked, he noticed a monk tending the ground in the fields beside the road. The monk said, "Good day," to the traveller, who nodded to the monk.

The traveller then turned to the monk and said, "Excuse me, do you mind if I ask you a question?"

"Not at all," replied the monk.

"I am travelling from the village in the mountains to the village in the valley, and I was wondering if you knew what it is like in the village in the valley."

"Tell me," said the monk, "What was your experience of the village in the mountains?"

"Dreadful," replied the traveller, "to be honest I am glad to be away from there. I found the people most unwelcoming. When I first arrived, I was greeted coldly. I was never made to feel part of the village no matter how hard I tried. The villagers keep very much to themselves, and they don't talk kindly to strangers. So tell me, what can I expect in the village in the valley?"

"I am sorry to tell you," said the monk, "but I think your experience will be very much the same there."

The traveller hung his head despondently and walked on.

A little while later, another traveller was journeying down the same road and he also came upon the monk.

"I'm going to the village in the valley," said the second traveller, "Do you know what it is like?"

"I do," replied the monk. "But first, tell me, where have you come from?"

"I've come from the village in the mountains."

"And how was that?"

"It was a wonderful experience. I would have stayed if I could, but I am committed to travelling on. I felt as though I was a member of the family in the village. The elders gave me much advice, the children laughed and joked with me, and people were generally kind and generous. I am sad that I had to leave from there. It will always hold special memories for me. And what of the village in the valley?" he asked again.

"I think you will find it much the same," replied the monk, "Good day to you."

"Good day and thank you," the traveller replied, smiled, and went on his way.

Attitude is everything. It governs the way you perceive the world and the way the world perceives you. It speaks volumes about you and your life. Your attitude forms the basis of everything that you do. It is a measure for your success and happiness.

The journey of life is not always a smooth ride. It is full of upheavals, confusions, and uncertainties. You may go through hard times feeling hurt, dejection, and emotional and physical pain. There are situations when you may feel out of control. But you have fortunately been given the power of choice. The key is to realize that it is not what happens to you that matters; it is how you choose to respond. The only difference between a good day and a bad day is your attitude towards it.

There are two categories of people I have seen. One is those who think 'I can' and the other one is 'I can't.' The people who belong to the first category are always focused on solutions, goals, achievement, and dream fulfilment. The second category people are more focused on obstacles, problems, imperfections, and flaws.

The 'I can' people will be always be happy, positive, and celebrating life. You will find these people humming and whistling while they are working or carrying out even the most routine chores; whereas the 'I can't' people will be in a foul mood, grumbling all the time. Where is the difference? Do the first set of people have everything they are looking for in their life? Nope, they don't. It's the way they look at things; and how you look at things is your attitude.

The first step to a journey, a dream, or a destination starts with your attitude. I remember the famous quote of Henry Ford, "Whether you think you can, or you think you can't - you're right."

Let's say you have to climb a mountain peak. You have two choices - you can either look at your goal, the mountain peak, decide to get there and start walking. Or you can just 'wish' to reach the peak while worrying about the jagged rocks along the way, deliberating about slipping and falling on them, and eventually forgetting about the peak because it's too risky.

Though the right attitude is vital for leading a successful life, the next question is whether it possible to have a positive attitude all the time. Well, my answer is that it may not be possible, but it can be worked on. All of us have our phases of highs and lows. We have to go through the grind every day and we are subjected to high pressures, both at work and as well as in maintaining our lifestyle, health, relationships, and many other things. We go through all kinds of stress all the time. But the fact still remains that it's only the right attitude that can take us towards our dreams and help us achieve them. So it is possible to change our attitude? Yes, certainly!

One of the definite ways is through the practice of gratitude; by adopting an 'attitude of gratitude' in life. It brings an instant shift within. You will start looking at life and its issues in a different light. There are innumerable things to be grateful for in your life. Feeling grateful or expressing gratitude ushers in a lot of positive energy, launching you in the direction of your goals and dreams. At any time, if you feel that there is nothing to be grateful for, check your pulse - if you feel it, you are alive and have a life of opportunities waiting for you. Having the right kind of attitude is the key to success in all ventures.

## WELL DONE IS BETTER THAN WELL SAID

You'll find plenty of people who'll keep talking about everything they wish to do, but don't really act upon them. There is an Irish proverb which says, "Turning it over in your mind won't plough the field." In network marketing, thinking about prospecting is not the same as doing it. Action is very important. So once you have sorted it in your mind, put it on paper and act in the real world. Make a schedule that you need to follow. It is easier to get things done when you have a discipline to follow instead of taking random action in any direction. Block out a certain time each week for prospecting and stick to it.

There are two main road blocks for taking the first step – lethargy and hesitancy.

I have heard of something called the law of diminishing intent, which says, "The more the time between your intention of doing a particular thing and your actually doing it, the greater are the chances that you won't do it." Once you take the first step, it is much easier. The path to achieve your dreams is a three-step process:

1.  *Write your dreams so that you know them.*

2.  *Communicate them to others, so you are committed to them.*

3.  *Now act on them so you can fulfil them.*

## DON'T MAKE THE BUSINESS A PART OF YOUR LIFE - MAKE IT YOUR LIFE

The mistake a lot of people make is that they forget the vital element of the business, which is YOU. This is a people's business and you are the building block. Yes, it is important to follow your upline and be a good student of the business, but more importantly, follow your own dreams with a passion.

Most of the time you have to pay a heavy price to make money in life, and that price is your personal happiness. I feel happiness should not be traded for money at all, because being happy is also your ultimate goal. Hence it becomes a bad bargain.

When you enter the business of network marketing, you will find a lot of other people cheering as well as inspiring you. This is the business of building a better you. Success and a good lifestyle are merely the by-products. When you are doing the right things, success will invariably be yours. Instead of running behind success, let it run after you. Invest in yourself.

## DO IT TODAY

If you are handed over the keys of your dream car today, would you try it out tomorrow? No, you would hop into it this very instant and start driving. Do the same for your business. Don't wait for things to happen - make them happen. Sitting for an extra hour with your mentor showing them an additional plan could make all the difference to your network and business. So, start today!

## TAKEAWAY

- *Attitude is everything. It governs the way you perceive the world and the way the world perceives you.*

- *The first step to a journey, a dream, or a destination starts with your attitude.*

- *In network marketing, thinking about prospecting is not the same as doing it. Action is very important.*

- *Having the right kind of attitude is the key to success in all ventures.*

*Chapter 14*

# THE BUSINESS OF RELATIONSHIPS

"Anything, everything, little or big becomes an adventure when the right person shares it. Nothing, nothing, nothing is worthwhile when we have to do it all alone."

**~ Kathleen Norris**

One of my friends worked for a company as their sales manager. His job profile required him to meet the procurement heads of various companies. He was selected as the 'apple candidate' of his company (shortlisted to be trained for the highest position in the company), and was much loved by his seniors and his customers alike. He was always ahead of his annual targets. Within no time he rapidly climbed the ladder of success.

Once, when we met over coffee, I asked him, "What is the secret to your success? You must be working really hard to fulfil your targets." What he shared was an eye-opener. "I never work more than the stipulated time, and neither do I focus on the sales. What I focus on are the people I deal with. Sales are just the by-product of my relationships with them. I love connecting with people. My customers already know my product. They just want to be sure that they are dealing with the right person."

Going by this philosophy, my friend has not only made some valuable relationships, but has also earned good money and a great reputation in the market.

We all are emotional beings. We all have the need to be heard and to be loved and cared for. Don't you feel good when somebody greets you with a cheerful good morning, or expresses gratitude for what you have done for them, or just wishes you well? These are small gestures, but they touch your heart. This is how human connections are established. And the heart-to-heart connections go a long way in establishing amazing and bonding relationships.

One of the great ways to connect with people is through their passion. Suppose you are meeting someone for the first time and you learn that their passion is music. You can instantly strike a chord with that person when you start discussing music, even if you don't know much about it. By doing so, you create a foundation for a long-term relationship and you also gain some knowledge about music in the process. As a result, it empowers you both.

One has to always remember that lasting relationships are always built on trust and honesty. Since we are emotional beings, anything fake gets easily caught by our heart, and the heart never lies. Genuine concern, love, or care can easily be felt.

Though this is the basis for building trusting relationships in any business, it is particularly important in network marketing because this business is all about connecting with people. The business of networking has been badly misunderstood. People often think that it is the business of selling, but let me tell you that it is the business of caring. If you let people know that you genuinely care for them, half the business is done already.

In network marketing, people keep bragging about their lists, saying, "I got 10 people," or "I got 20 people," but it is really important to ask yourself whether you really care about each person you have in your list, or whether you are trying to push the business down the throat of that person even if he or she doesn't need it. Do you just want to increase your list, or do you want to make some beautiful relationships? Suppose you meet someone in the elevator and you get talking and you strike a chord. That person need not appear in your list at all, but you have created an opportunity to create a friendship which may later turn into a serious business relationship.

Another important virtue that network marketing teaches us is that of working as a team. Michael Jordan once said, "Talent wins games, but teamwork and intelligence wins championships." This applies to the game of network marketing as well. You might have plenty of uplines and downlines who are supremely talented, but if you all cannot work as a cohesive unit, you are calling for trouble and collapse of your talent pool. So what can you do to keep your troops together and complete the mission of achieving your dreams? Take note of the following.

## THIS BUSINESS IS PERSONAL

It has been said numerous times by numerous people that network marketing is a business of relationships. On one hand, you have to be a role model for your downlines, while on the other you learn all you can from your uplines. You need to empathize to nurture the relationships you have built. Coaching, counselling, and mentoring are all critical to this business. You have to be able to give and receive all these three elements.

Remember that you, your uplines, and your downlines are all students of the same university. You are students throughout your life. This actually lifts a load off your shoulders, as it gives you the safe space to be yourself and make mistakes. Thus learning becomes easy. Rather than playing superhero, it makes better sense to stick to your core competency. Where needed, also have the courage to acknowledge that you may not know about something, and be bold enough to face it.

## LIFETIME VALIDITY

You always heard of this expression for products and services. It holds true for network marketing as well. This business is all about people and their empowerment. Once you get a signup, it's a person you are building a relationship with. You are not just building your business, but a bond that goes well beyond it. Bring the relationship to a stage where your downline can call you lifelong, be it for any hurdles in the business or anything apart from that. The most beautiful aspect of network marketing is that all in the network grow together and there is no pressure or one-upmanship. This in turn provides a healthy space for everyone to grow at their own pace.

# PEOPLE DON'T CARE HOW MUCH YOU KNOW, THEY WANT TO KNOW HOW MUCH YOU CARE

Unlike traditional businesses, you are not dealing here with raw materials, machinery, capital, debts, investments, debit, credit, or balance sheets. You are dealing with people who are driven by emotions. The key is to understand each emotion and make decisions with your heart rather than with your mind. I disagree when people say that nothing is at stake when it comes to network marketing and question why people should be emotional. The truth is that your dream and your reason to do the business are at stake, and for me, nothing is bigger or comes closer to it. More so, because your job is never going to achieve all your dreams, and maybe your traditional business will give you the money, but not the time to enjoy your financial freedom.

## COMPASSION PRECEDES PASSION

Yes, you must be passionate about the business. And it's good to be motivated – it's great that you want to show more plans and prospect more people. However, you're missing a point. You are going to make it big only when you begin understanding others in your team. I say this because your dreams are interlinked with the dreams of others in your team. So make every move keeping others in mind as well, not just yourself.

## BE A PEOPLE PERSON

There is no other business in the world other than network marketing, which can rightly claim that it is of the people, by the people, and for the people. Yes, there are products and services offered through various distribution channels in the business, but those are inconsequential when you compare them to the earning potential and the lifestyle that you can enjoy.

Treat it as a people's business and the people in your team will make their dreams come true, which in turn will result in the fulfilment of your own dreams. If people don't accept you, they won't accept what you are saying. Between a ready prospect and a great business opportunity stands a person, and that person is you. The business is great and the prospect is ready, the rest is up to you.

## TAKEAWAY

- *We all are emotional beings. We all have the need to be heard and to be loved and cared for.*

- *Heart-to-heart connections go a long way in establishing amazing and bonding relationships.*

- *This business is all about people and their empowerment.*

- *You need to empathize to nurture the relationships you have built.*

- *Coaching, counselling, and mentoring are all critical to this business.*

- *You are dealing with people who are driven with emotions. The key is to understand each emotion and make decisions with your heart rather than with your mind.*

- *You are going to make it big only when you begin understanding others in your team.*

*Chapter 15*

# LEADING LEADERS

"Be the change you want to see in the world."
**– Mahatma Gandhi**

One day, a lady came to see Mahatma Gandhi along with her 10-year-old son. She met with Gandhiji and said, "My son has a bad habit of eating too much of jaggery [an unrefined sugar]. I have been asking him to give up this habit, but he does not listen to me. Sir, the whole nation listens to you. I am sure my son will definitely follow your advice. Can you please instruct him not to eat excessive jaggery?"

Mahatma Gandhi thought for a while and asked the lady to bring her son again after a week. As requested, the lady returned the next week along with her son. Mahatma Gandhi put his hand on the head of the boy and told him, "My dear child, don't eat too much jaggery. It can be harmful to your health." The voice and tone left no room for doubt and it had a strong impact on the young lad.

The puzzled lady, however, asked in confusion, "Gandhiji, I don't understand. You could have told him the same thing last week itself. Why did you make us come back after a week?"

Gandhiji told the lady, "I myself used to frequently eat jaggery until last week. I needed a week's time to quit eating jaggery so that I could speak to your son with conviction."

One needs to lead by example rather than having double standards: expecting the world of other people, whilst doing very little oneself. A true leader walks his talk and practices in his own life what he preaches to others.

## LEADERSHIP IN NETWORK MARKETING

The word 'leader' has a very different connotation in the world of network marketing. Unlike most other industries, you cannot join here as a leader. A person can finish an MBA and be hired in a multinational company as a general manager, but it is not like that in network marketing. Every leader starts at the same place - at the bottom of the ladder - and goes up by building the business.

Most companies have different terms for leaders at various levels, and by virtue of that term, everyone in the company knows just how much that person has achieved. The key difference in leadership in network marketing is that you are leading free people here. Each person in your network is free, which is why the term 'free enterprise' came into being. Here, you will find that the people you lead are following simply because you add value to their lives and because they believe in you - not because they have to.

## A GOOD FOLLOWER CAN BE A GOOD LEADER

The Greek philosopher and scientist Aristotle once said, "He who cannot be a good follower cannot be a good leader."

To be a good leader, one has to be a good follower; but every good follower need not necessarily be a good leader.

In my opinion, a good follower is the one who takes the responsibility of carrying the job across the finish line and who always looks for ways to make the process better. They don't need to be told about the jobs to be completed and they are very dependable. They are good at taking orders, are humble and disciplined, and have integrity.

A good leader, on the other hand, knows where he is headed to, understands the purpose and objectives, and has a clear vision of the ultimate goal that he and his group wish to attain. A good leader fully dedicates himself to achieve that goal ethically. A good leader inspires people to have confidence in him. A good leader inspires them to have confidence in themselves.

The followers will always follow the leader, though not entirely. Whatever the leader does right, the group generally may do half as right. And whatever the leader does wrong, the group may do twice as wrong. In network marketing, people struggle to get followers. The secret is not simply being good and getting people to follow you. Being a good leader is more about developing yourself – working on yourself and raising yourself to such a level that people would want to follow you. Leadership is responsibility, not authority.

Here are some key points:

## DON'T BE A BOSS, BE A LEADER

"Do unto others what you would want them to do to you." The best part about network marketing is that you do not have a boss. But it can also be a great weakness because you have no pressure and no obligation to report to anyone. Therefore, it is important to create a culture where you do business as a leader and talk like a friend. This means you take everyone on board rather than set stringent goals that burden your downlines with unreasonable expectations.

Because leadership comes with so much responsibility, your choices are narrowed. You cannot do what you feel like doing, but you rather do what you are meant to do. You have fewer liberties because the progress of so many people is linked to yours. Don't just be a leader – give birth to other leaders as well. Make yourself a leader that people wish to replicate and help them become leaders themselves, so that you can have a team that has multiple leaders. Instil in your team the best practices as well as the confidence to handle situations so that they don't quit in the face of problems and obstacles but are rather geared to deal with them. This is a people's business and it demands not only for you to lead, but also to empower others to lead.

## STEER YOUR TEAM TO SUCCESS

Your team is looking at you as a role model, and is also looking at you to set the direction. In order to be a coach and a mentor, you need to keep growing yourself, not only in terms of business, but also as a person. Commit to growing at a personal level, so that you are staying one step ahead at all times. Give the team a direction, and steer your team to success. Make decisions when needed and have the humility to say "I will check with my upline," if required.

Understand the people in your team, including their strengths and weaknesses. When they see you following systems and being honest, they will be inspired to follow the same.

## WHAT DOES IT TAKE TO BE A GOOD UPLINE?

In network marketing, it is seen that the upline is often put on a pedestal. The upline usually becomes a role model for the downline. In the process, people often look up to their upline not only for product and business knowledge, but also for personal advice. They also expect the upline to behave in a certain way, do certain things, and to be always right in whatever they do. The problem occurs when the upline cannot live up to their prejudiced expectations. The downline needs to remember that the person who introduced them to the business is also a human, and all humans have their shortcomings. It is important for the downline to grant them the space to be human.

A person who learns well can teach well. To be a great upline, one has to be a good downline. Each person will have his own strengths and weaknesses. Even the best uplines may have faults. One needs to go beyond those imperfections and appreciate the positives in that person.

Some of the qualities that define a good upline are:

- *Having faith in the downline.*
- *Motivating the downline to achieve their true potential.*

- *Sharing his success with his downline, and giving them the confidence that if he can do it, so can they.*

- *Edifying their achievements.*

- *Developing a relation with the downline and also valuing that relationship.*

- *Guiding the downline in the right direction and always walking the talk.*

- *Being completely transparent in financial dealings and not indulging in any unethical practices.*

To sum it in a single word, a good upline cares for the downline. Be an exceptional leader and inspire many people in the field of network marketing.

## TAKEAWAY

- *A true leader walks his talk and practices in his own life what he preaches to others.*

- *The beauty of network marketing is that every leader starts at the same place - at the bottom of the ladder - and goes up by building the business.*

- *Each person in your network is free, which is why the term 'free enterprise' came into being.*

- *The best part about network marketing is that you do not have a boss.*

- *In order to be a coach and a mentor, you need to keep developing yourself, not only in terms of business but also as a person.*

*Chapter 16*

# MENTORING

"If you light a lamp for someone, it will also brighten your own path."

**– Gautama Buddha**

Aristotle, the famous philosopher, was invited by King Philip of Greece to become the tutor to his son Alexander in 343 BC. He taught him the poems of Homer, which inspired Alexander's great love for literature. It is said that Aristotle gave Alexander him his annotated copy of Homer's The Iliad, a book that Alexander considered a handbook on the art of war. He had this book by his side during his legendary conquests.

During Alexander's remarkable march throughout the world, his love for books, instilled in him by Aristotle, led him to start collecting them. Aristotle encouraged Alexander toward Eastern conquest. He counselled Alexander to be a leader to the Greeks and be a despot to the barbarians, and to look after his army like friends and relatives. Aristotle taught him Greek, Hebrew, Babylonian, and Latin. He equipped him with knowledge about the nature of the sea and the wind, the course of the stars, and the lifespan of the world. The great teacher also showed his royal student the meaning of justice and taught him oratory skills. He also warned him against the wiles of 'loose women.'

It was this mentoring that moulded young Alexander into what the world remembers him as — Alexander the Great.

This is the power of mentoring. Yes, Alexander would have been a king even without the help of Aristotle, but not the legend that that world remembers him as. A mentor is someone who can push you to the next level.

Who is a mentor and what exactly is mentoring? A mentor is defined as a wise and trusted guide, an advisor. Mentoring is an important leadership quality. It involves making your experience available to another individual to help that person grow using the benefit of your experience. This could be at a professional as well as a personal level. In order to be a good mentor, you not only need to understand others, but you need to first understand yourself and know what your own strengths are. Mentoring others is a gift of both time and service.

Michael Jordan, the famous basketball player, was mentored by Dean Smith, who was also his coach. Michael Jordan gives a lot of credit of his success to his mentor when he says, "Other than my parents, no one had a bigger influence on my life than Coach Smith. He was more than a coach – he was my mentor, my teacher, my second father. He was always there for me whenever I needed him and I loved him for it. In teaching me the game of basketball, he taught me about life."

Bill Gates, one of the richest people in the world, duly credits part of his success to his mentor, the businessman and investor Warren Buffet. During an interview with CBC, Gates credited Buffet for teaching him how to deal with tough situations and how to think long-term. Gates also greatly admires Buffet's "desire to teach things that are complex and put them in a simple form, so that people can understand and get the benefit of all his experience."

Over the years, influential men and women have been making a profound influence on many lives by being their mentors.

The network marketing business relies very strongly on the principle of mentoring. Free enterprise, unlike a corporate office, does not have someone watching over you over their shoulder all the time. While this allows you to have your space, it also gives you the freedom to make a lot of mistakes. Within the framework of freedom, mentoring plays a key role in ensuring that you stay on track.

One key trait of mentoring is that it cannot be imposed. The mentee needs to request for it. It works best when the mentee approaches the mentor and asks for guidance. A good mentor has the capacity to fuel the desire in his mentee and push him to make it to the top. While mentoring helps the person being advised, it can also be a rewarding experience for the person offering it. Teaching is one of the best forms of learning, and while helping another person grow, you learn to see things with a fresh perspective.

In the corporate world, mentoring is not as common, because people are insecure as they think that if they teach another person in their team to grow, that person may become a threat to the mentor's own job position. However, there is no such threat in network marketing. Good mentoring relies on various functions — building trust, assessing situations, coaching, and counselling. Success is not circumstantial.

Every person has the potential to succeed, and often people just need someone to recognize that spark and fan it into a flame. A good mentor is one who sees the spark.

## KEY QUALITIES OF AN EFFECTIVE MENTOR

A mentor-mentee pairing requires work, commitment, and follow-through on both sides if it's going to succeed. There has to be genuine caring for the well-being of the mentee from the mentor's side. Only then will the mentee feel confident about sharing their life with the mentor. They will be open to the advice and will trust it. Here are some points to note.

Understanding the mentee: The mentor needs to thoroughly understand the mentee first - who is he, what is his mental makeup, what is his current status, what are his aspirations, and so on. If the mentor starts mentoring without a basic understanding of what kind of a person his mentee is, every step or piece of advice thereafter will go in vain. In network marketing, when the downline looks at the upline for mentoring, it is critical that the upline understands the place his downline is coming from and that he forms the advice suited to that person and situation.

Trust: Trust is the foundation of any relationship and business. One needs to be trustworthy. A good mentor will respect the trust bestowed upon him by the mentee and will keep the confidentiality. He will never indulge in any kind of gossip. He will put you at ease and create a safe space where you feel secure to discuss about your issues. In networking, when the trust is lost over one person, it is likely that the entire downline will get affected.

Big-heartedness: This is essential. A great mentor wants you to succeed, and he will actively support your success with words and action. A great mentor would never be envious or feel threatened by your growth; he would rather congratulate you on your triumphs and help you recover from your setbacks. The generous mentor would make connections or offer resources that could be useful to you whenever he can. Most important, a generous mentor believes in your potential and communicates that to you freely and with hope. The generous mentor supports you to become the person you want to become. There is nothing to lose in this relationship. It is always a win-win situation.

Approachability and availability: A good mentor makes you feel comfortable when you approach for advice or consultation; however, the mentee should not pile all his problems upon him and take the mentor for granted. So, it's good policy to establish a set day and time for regular sessions or meetings. And once these time parameters are established, both mentor and mentee must stick to their commitments wholeheartedly and be ready to listen well and with an open mind.

Look at the iceberg: A good mentor can see the tip of the iceberg and understand that there is more to it. The trick is to understand the symptom and find out where the root cause of the problem is. Once that is reached, he can give a real solution.

Empower the mentee: Being a mentor means making an important, serious commitment to someone, so a good mentor gives the mentee - and the process - the respect he or she deserves. He shows faith in the mentee's abilities and in the process by preparing for each mentoring session. Yes, it's important for the mentee to actively participate and even take the lead in these sessions. But he should ask the mentee what topics or subjects he or she wants to talk about beforehand, and the mentor should outline the key points he wants to focus on ahead of time and should have a plan ready for imparting the details in an effective and efficient way.

Bring out the best: A mentor needs to act as a facilitator and not impose his views, suggestions, and solutions on the mentee. People are more apt to follow solutions that they have 'discovered' rather than those they have been offered. Just leading people in the right direction often helps them find their answers.

Act out of wisdom: In today's digital age, knowledge is easily, freely, and abundantly available. But there is a difference between knowledge and wisdom. Wisdom comes only from experience, after assimilating and inculcating the lessons you learnt. For example, if you go a certain way and you fall, you can make another person who is walking through the same path aware of the danger.

They say that experience is the best teacher. Some people simply don't spend much time thinking about their own experience; a person can be quite knowledgeable and successful without having reflected much on how they got to where they are today. However, just hearing about what someone has done is much less valuable than hearing about why they did it and about their understanding of why it worked or didn't work. The insight given by the mentor can help the mentee avoid pitfalls in life.

A mentee who in turn edifies his mentor with others has power over his mentor by virtue of that edification. The mentee's belief in his mentor puts a lot of responsibility on the mentor to ensure the mentee's success.

A mistake that people often make is to ask for opinions and advice from those who have no interest in their growth. In network marketing, the best practice is to take the obstacle and go to the upline. The issue could be that "the products are expensive," or "I don't show a good plan," or "Whenever I show the plan there are too many objections," or "I make the connect, but people don't show up."

It is good to have a mentor who can guide you and help you find solutions to these issues.

Mentoring and being able to take care of your team is an indispensible quality needed to succeed. Make sure people show up not by force, but by will. This builds comradery. Be accountable. Never indulge in gossip about other businesses, because the success or failure of that will impact this business as well.

In network marketing, having a mentor can be helpful, but having a mentor who is trustworthy, big-hearted, wise, approachable, and understanding can be life-altering. A mentor and mentee can hold hands and together walk the path of success and achieve their dreams without posing any threat to each other.

## TAKEAWAY

- *Mentoring involves making your experience available to another individual to help that person grow using the benefit of your experience.*

- *Over the years, influential men and women have been making a profound influence on many lives by being their mentors.*

- *A mentor-mentee pairing requires work, commitment, and follow-through on both sides if it's going to succeed.*

- *Trust is the foundation of any relationship or business.*

- *A mentor needs to act as a facilitator and not impose his views, suggestions, and solutions on the mentee.*

- *In network marketing, having a mentor can be helpful, but having a mentor who is trustworthy, big-hearted, wise, approachable, and understanding can be life-altering.*

*Chapter 17*

# ARE YOU A GOOD NETWORKER?

"A network replaces the weakness of the
individual with the strength of the group."
**~ Harvey Mackey**

In today's rapidly changing world, it is seen that
networking plays a role more important than ever
before in the history of mankind. Social networking
sites like Facebook, LinkedIn, Twitter, Instagram,
Whatsapp, and the like have brought forth an
incredible revolution. We have started using these
media for almost everything, from something as
routine as shopping or connecting with friends to
something as serious as looking for a job or bringing
about social reform. Whenever my friend's daughter
wants to bake a cake, she simply asks her friends on
Facebook for a recipe and she is instantly equipped
with ten different cake recipes. Another friend told
me that he found a publisher on LinkedIn for his
forthcoming book. Undoubtedly, networking has
become an integral part of our everyday lives. We
are networking all the time. The question is, to what
extent do we use this?

The key to success in network marketing is
NETWORKING. You will find that you can use the
skills gained from this business in virtually every

other aspect of your life as well. People who succeed in life are people like you and me, who happen to possess excellent networking skills. These networkers achieve extraordinary results because they team up with other ordinary people and leverage their time and ability. To put it simply, a network is a group of people communicating and sharing their ideas, data, contacts, and resources to achieve the compounded benefit for an entire network. Each person contributes their own share to get the support and experience of a large group.

## TIPS FOR POWER NETWORKING

**Make real contacts:** The Internet has taken networking to a new level, where people tweet and post many times every day. With cell phones and social networking sites we can have innumerable 'friends.' However, a lot of these so-called relations are generally shallow because you often have people on your group whom you don't really know. To reap more benefit, select people with common interests and people who will add value by virtue of being in your network.

**Use social networking:** It is the digital age, and the number of people you can meet on the Internet is huge and the potential it holds cannot be ignored. However, it is easy to get overwhelmed with the numbers and get into a pattern of spending too much time in the virtual world. Build a LinkedIn or Facebook page that defines your interests and post articles communicating your interests and inclination to people.

**Circulate to percolate:** With due respect to social media, physically meeting people definitely builds stronger, more lasting bonds. Find associations, clubs, meetings, and groups where you can find like-minded people. For example, you may be part of a reading club because you like to read, and you can easily build networks with other readers who share a common ground with you in their passion for books. Walk up to such people and talk to them. People often want to talk, but are hesitant to be the first one to break the ice. You will find most people are actually looking for someone to talk to.

**Ask open-ended questions in networking conversations:** Get the conversations going. Ask 'who, what, where, when, why, how' questions that lead to a conversation. Look for what you have in common with the other person. An example could be the host, the weather, a television show - anything that builds common ground. Once you have put forward the question, let the other person speak. Listen. People prefer to talk.

**Quickly connect with referrals from friends:** When you do this, you show respect to the person who referred you. When they see people benefiting from their referrals, they are happy to give you more leads.

**Nurture the relationships you value:** Relationships are investments. You only 'relate' to people who share some common ground with you. You have to invest time and energy in developing and nurturing those relationships. Communication is key. Stay in touch from time to time for your relationship to grow.

## WHAT TO AVOID?

**Overwhelming the person with too many details**: Sometimes we get so carried away speaking to a person that we forget to check if they are still interested. Do not go into unnecessary details that could put off the other person.

**Interrogation:** Asking questions that lead to some common topics of interests to set the conversation going is good, but be extremely careful not to step into the interrogative mode. No one really likes to be interrogated, wouldn't you agree? Too many questions coming too fast may give that feeling. Networking is not aggressive or mechanical. It's about taking a genuine interest in people.

**Interrupting:** Don't interrupt people. We all like to finish a story we have started or a point we are making. An interruption breaks a cycle of thought and communication.

**Selling things:** While networking, you are making a connection. This is a business of sharing information, and there are great tools that'll help you present the products or services and business to your candidates. All you do is work with those who are interested. The business will thus happen. Being good at selling things is a bonus, though.

**Have a story to tell:** People can relate to real-life stories. Let them infer the message from your story. Sometimes, people have the misconception that they are doing very well in the networking business, but let me tell you that they are most often barely scraping their potential which is limited by the size of their dreams. Here is an apt example of limited dreams. I recently met a couple at a function who were very proficient in their field, and both were holding very high positions. They were unhappy about the fact that they were stuck in their positions and were not compensated enough. They felt that the company should change their plans so that they could get what they deserved.

So I asked them to write down their dreams. "Don't tell me," I said. "You built it up to this level, right? And it is phenomenal. I am sure you had a dream back then which got you here. So now that you are here, you must be having dreams for the future. It could be a good idea to write them down."

The couple spent some time deliberating, and what came through is that they both had a dream and that dream had only brought them up to this point. They were already living their restricted dream and they could not progress because they had not created new dreams.

## Edification is the key

Your prospects will never take you seriously till your downlines edify you as a leader or game-changer. If you are the leader of your team then there needs to be an aura of credibility and trust built around you because whatever you give to others comes back to you many times over. It goes without saying that you need to do exactly the same for your seniors. Remember certain key gestures before a plan.

- *When you see your upline who is about to show a plan to your prospect, always get up from your chair and greet him. By giving more respect to your upline, you establish his credibility as a leader. Thereafter, whatever he states is received with more attention by your prospect. In short, the more credibility and respect you build for your upline, the more respect he will earn from your prospect.*

- *An important thing: you do need to edify your upline or leader, but NEVER lie, because when your lie is caught, everything that you have ever stated comes into question - about the leader, about the business, or about yourself, including the truths.*

- *Before your upline enters the venue, talk highly of your upline to the prospect. This is important because when the prospect meets your upline, he or she should give him his full attention.*

- *Sit on the edge. Be alert. Don't be too relaxed. Maintain eye contact, smile, give a nod, switch off your cell phone, and take notes when your mentor is speaking. Be in the present moment, and listen intently. Laugh even if you have heard the joke before, because you are setting an example for the prospect. Remember, as mentioned earlier, they will do half the good things you do.*

- *Look sharp. Let people take you seriously. You feel a lot more confident when you know you are well-dressed and well-groomed. It's much easier to make a positive impression on people when looking sharp.*

- *Be punctual. Don't take people's time for granted. People respect someone who values their time just like his own. Time is money, after all.*

- *Have an uplifting vocabulary: what you speak shows you for who you are and reflects where you are going to be. It's not only about what you say but also about how you say it.*

- *Stay positive and deal with the negative: as a leader, it is your job to become a diffuser. If there is a negative situation brewing, you, as a leader, should be able to step in and diffuse that situation.*

- *Learn how to conduct yourself when things go wrong. Don't make irreversible key decisions when hungry, angry, or tired. These are all important nuances which can make or break a plan – and, for that matter, a leader as well.*

Although we need to understand that we are all humans with imperfections, we have a huge potential to achieve our dreams. Ultimately, what really matters is one's attitude towards things. Change your vocabulary to one that spells 'success.' If you want to achieve success in network marketing, replace the words 'frustrated,' 'overwhelmed,' and 'dejected' from your vocabulary with more positive ones. Stop creating negative experiences in your life and you will see a huge transformation in and around you.

Network marketing offers a huge potential for you to grow and help others grow with you.

## TAKEAWAY

- *The key to success in network marketing is networking.*

- *To put it simply, a network is a group of people communicating and sharing their ideas, data, contacts, and resources to achieve the compounded benefit for an entire network.*

- *It is a digital age and the number of people you can meet on the internet is huge, and the potential it holds cannot be ignored.*

- *Your prospects will never take you seriously till your downlines edify you as a leader or a game changer.*

- *When they see people benefiting from their referrals, they are happy to give you more leads.*

- *Sometimes we get so carried away speaking to a person that we forget to check if he is still interested.*

- *The more credibility and respect you build for your upline, the more respect he will earn from your prospect.*